She should be happy being best friends with Milo. Her heart had skipped around him for years, but she'd always managed to put it back in its place. Maybe coming back to California was a mistake. But she'd felt called here, like she needed to come home—at least for a little while.

It was a feeling she still couldn't explain, but Quinn had always chosen new locations and jobs by what felt right. And working with Milo had felt right. So why was it so hard?

Turning on the shower, Quinn quickly stripped off her scrubs and tried to push away the thoughts of the man just outside the door.

How did Milo kiss? She shivered despite the heat of the water on her skin. She wanted an answer to that question—desperately.

Dear Reader,

One of my favorite romance tropes has always been best friends to lovers. There is something special about realizing that your friend is the one your heart belongs to. Quinn and Milo have a deep friendship, but each craves so much more.

Certified nurse-midwife Quinn Davis has never really felt at home. She's traveled the world but still hasn't found her place. But when she returns to Los Angeles to work with her best friend, sparks fly. Can home really be the place she's avoided for so long?

Dr. Milo Russell has always admired Quinn's ability to go with her gut. But Milo needs what the security plans, outlines and goal sheets give him. However, when Quinn challenges him to think about what he really wants, Milo realizes the answer is her! Can he convince his wonderful, impulsive best friend that the dream he desires most is her heart?

I hope you enjoy getting to know these two best friends turned soul mates as much as I enjoyed writing them.

Happy reading!

Juliette Hyland

A STOLEN KISS
WITH THE MIDWIFE

———

JULIETTE HYLAND

HARLEQUIN

MEDICAL
ROMANCE

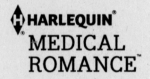

HARLEQUIN®
MEDICAL
ROMANCE™

Recycling programs
for this product may
not exist in your area.

ISBN-13: 978-1-335-40432-9

A Stolen Kiss with the Midwife

Copyright © 2021 by Juliette Hyland

This edition published by arrangement with Harlequin Books S.A.

For questions and comments about the quality of this book,
please contact us at CustomerService@Harlequin.com.

Harlequin Enterprises ULC
22 Adelaide St. West, 40th Floor
Toronto, Ontario M5H 4E3, Canada
www.Harlequin.com

Printed in U.S.A.

Juliette Hyland began crafting heroes and heroines in high school. She lives in Ohio with her Prince Charming, who has patiently listened to many rants regarding characters failing to follow the outline. When not working on fun and flirty happily-ever-afters, Juliette can be found spending time with her beautiful daughters, giant dogs or sewing uneven stitches with her sewing machine.

Books by Juliette Hyland

Harlequin Medical Romance

Unlocking the Ex-Army Doc's Heart
Falling Again for the Single Dad

Visit the Author Profile page at Harlequin.com.

For my sister—my confidante and coconspirator.
Here's to more fun and crazy days!

CHAPTER ONE

CERTIFIED NURSE-MIDWIFE Quinn Davis refused to look out the window, even as a few of the other nurses gaped at the orange blaze on the horizon. The wildfire had been burning for almost three weeks; she didn't need to see the damage. Quinn knew what the fire looked like, knew where it was heading, knew what was at risk.

"I can't believe it's still burning."

"I heard it's less than fifteen percent contained."

"No! I was listening to the news this morning, but I changed the station before they talked numbers."

It was twenty percent contained. Quinn had been monitoring the blaze since it began, but she kept the news to herself. She didn't want to join the conversation. Didn't trust herself not to break.

If she could only drown out their words.

She had a patient in labor; she couldn't afford

to be distracted right now. At least, not distracted any further.

Quinn slid into a chair and tried to block Rhonda and Sherrie's exclamations from her ears. Both nurses commuted in from the south. This fire wouldn't touch them—not directly. But no one in this area of California ever truly believed a wildfire couldn't reach them.

Georgia stuck her head into the lounge. "Rhonda, Olivia is at nine centimeters."

"Guess that puts us on deck." Sherrie turned from the window and nodded to Quinn as she and Rhonda left to tend to their patient.

Quinn was grateful that work had called them away before they'd asked her about the destruction in the hills.

Or if she was worried.

Her phone pinged with a text message from her landlady, asking if she was safe. She managed to type a short affirmative without tearing up—barely. The evacuation notice for Quinn's neighborhood had shifted from voluntary to mandatory during her shift. A sob pressed against the back of Quinn's throat, but she refused to let it out.

Tapping her foot against the small table in the lounge, Quinn rolled her neck from side to side and tried to think of anything besides the bungalow being in the fire line.

It was just a place...

But it wasn't. The longest lease Quinn had ever signed before she'd seen the bungalow was for six months. During her decade as a traveling nurse, she'd lived out of two duffel bags. She didn't get attached to places—or to people. She'd learned the hard way that just because she connected didn't mean others did. Picking up and moving was ingrained in her.

Or, it had been, until the position at St. Brigit's had opened.

Maybe this was punishment for her giving in to the desire to finally claim something as her own. For painting walls and pretending the bungalow was really hers. *No!* She would not let her brain accept that possibility.

Quinn also refused to look at the opportunity to work with her best friend as anything other than a blessing.

She'd planned St. Brigit's to be a temporary place, too—a year-long contract at best—but something about that bungalow had called to her.

Or maybe it was being back in California.

When her landlady had told her she'd wanted a long-term tenant, Quinn had readily agreed.

Still, she hadn't bought new furniture. Renting had seemed safer. Easier to dispose of if things didn't work out.

Yet, the bungalow, even with its rented furnishings, had felt like hers. *A home.* She'd never felt at home anywhere, not even as a child. She'd seen so much of the world but never found a place to really call hers. It didn't make sense that it was happening here—the home she'd escaped as soon as she'd graduated college. But no matter how much Quinn pushed back, the seed of a possible forever here in California had refused to slow its bloom.

But now her home was turning to ash.

She swallowed against the tightness in her throat. The yearning for a home, a real home, was uncomfortable. Maybe her biological clock was ticking—a primal desire urging her to plant roots so she could start a family—but that seemed too superficial. Coming back to California had felt different than she'd expected.

She felt different.

Why now? There'd been upheaval in her life before. So many times. And it had never made her want a home or a family. Quinn shifted. Trying to find a comfortable position on the plastic lounge chair was a lost cause, and her body was restless.

She absently rubbed the skin on the finger of her left hand. She'd worn James's engagement ring for less than three weeks before he'd confessed to cheating on her with one of the other itinerant nurses. The worst part was that she hadn't even been all that surprised. Her birth mother hadn't wanted her. Quinn hadn't lived up to her adoptive parents' dreams—so why had she thought James would be different?

She hadn't been angry, hadn't yelled or thrown anything. Quinn couldn't even remember crying. She'd simply packed her bags and moved on. A wildfire in the hills of California—something she'd seen far too many times growing up—wasn't unexpected, but it was throwing her out of sync.

It was her own fault. She knew better than to surrender to sentiment.

Quinn bit her lip and wiped her hands on her thighs as she tried to push away the image of her home on fire. Squeezing her eyes closed, she crossed her arms and willed the tears away.

Before rushing into the birthing center last night, why hadn't she thought to grab the things she'd packed a week ago? She'd boxed the few items that she cared about and carefully stowed them where she could snatch them up in less than ten minutes if the evac orders came down. She should have brought them with her.

"If your face gets any longer…"

A hot cup of coffee pressed against her fingers and Quinn lifted it to her lips without opening her eyes. The black coffee was bitter, and a bit burned, but the caffeine kick was what she needed. And she was grateful for any distraction.

"Seriously, Quinn. What's going on?"

A knee connected with hers as Milo slid into

the chair across from her, and Quinn ignored the tingles that slid along her leg. She was tired, worried, and her emotions were tangled. That was the only reason she was reacting to Dr. Milo Russell this morning, she told herself, ignoring the fact that she'd felt those same tingles yesterday morning…and every other day since she'd walked into his arms at the airport eight months ago. Such a simple welcome that had shifted everything in Quinn's soul.

Almost a year later and she still couldn't explain the feelings.

Or why those emotions hadn't made her pack her bags and flee.

Luckily, Quinn's brain was too full of other worries to let that one take residency in the front of her mind today. Not that it ever wandered away for long, though…

Opening her eyes, Quinn tipped her cup at Milo as he took a seat beside her on the lounge chair. His jade eyes bore through her and she barely kept herself from leaning into him. Milo was her friend. Her best friend. He was the reason she'd leaped at the opportunity to work at St. Brigit's.

Sure, he was gorgeous. *Stunning.* His deep dimples were the stuff of legend. She'd heard more than one single lady talk about what it might take to get those dimples to appear outside the birthing center. But Quinn never swooned over anyone. Not over her cheating ex-fiancé and certainly not over Milo. At least, that had been true until she'd moved back to California. Now she yearned for any contact with him.

Quinn and Milo had always just been Quinn and Milo. They'd been best friends since grade school when Quinn had refused to name the person who had started the epic food fight. She'd stood in the principal's office, refusing to out the new kid, when Milo had marched in and declared that he'd thrown the first nugget. In truth, neither had thought tossing a few hard chicken nuggets would result in pandemonium and pudding on the walls—but they'd cleaned it together. And they'd had each other's backs ever since.

Even when wanderlust had taken her to the other side of the country or the other side of the world, she and Milo always kept in touch. Video calls, emails and social media had meant they were only ever a GIF away. He was the one constant in her rambling life. Always there to make her laugh, to bounce ideas off about her next move, to make her happy.

He'd always just been her friend Milo and working together at St. Brigit's was a first for them. She'd enjoyed every minute of it, even if she was in a constant battle to get her body to stop substituting friendly feelings with romantic ones.

"My neighborhood was placed under mandatory evac." She ignored the shake in her hand as she lifted the coffee cup to her lips again. One of the packed boxes was filled with pictures of her and Milo, his sister, and his mother. Diana Russell had never made Quinn feel unwelcome—despite being a single mom and a hardworking physician—unlike Quinn's own family. If that box of memories was lost... Quinn mentally kicked herself. She was *not* going to travel that well-worn path again this morning.

"Do you need to leave?" Milo leaned forward and the soft scent of his cedar shampoo blended with the smell of her coffee.

What was wrong with her? Before she'd returned to California, she couldn't have told anyone anything about Milo's shampoo. Though she could have told them that the scrunch of his nose meant he was concerned. And that a twitch in his left cheek meant he was holding in a laugh, but a twitch in his right cheek meant he was angry.

Maybe the lines between friends and more had blurred long ago...

They'd spent almost all their free time together since she'd arrived, enjoying the opportunity to be together in person rather than on the screen. He'd helped paint her bungalow, and they'd watched silly romantic comedies while sharing giant bowls of popcorn. But he'd never mentioned wanting more.

And Milo always knew what he wanted.

Focus!

Shaking her head, Quinn shrugged. "Molly's in labor. You know her history." Molly had struggled with infertility, and she and her partner had had more than their share of losses over the past five years. After so many disappointments, they'd adopted a son a few years ago—a gorgeous little boy they were both devoted to—and had been stunned when she had conceived naturally.

"I think Molly would understand." Milo gripped her fingers.

The simple gesture made Quinn's heart rate pick up, but she didn't pull away. She didn't have the strength to put distance between them today—even if she wanted to. Glancing out the window, she shuddered. "If I left right now, I wouldn't make it home before the roads closed. I'm just mad I didn't throw stuff in the car before I left last night."

She forced her gaze away from the orange glow creeping along the hills. Her home was really in danger. The place she'd felt called to might vanish.

"Why not?" Milo's lips formed a soft smile that any other day would have sent her belly tumbling with need. "The reports coming in—" He caught his final words.

She knew all about the reports. Knew that if it had been Milo's home, he'd have already prepared a five-page emergency plan. Heck, he probably had one anyway.

Her chest constricted. Plans provided safety and security. But they could be weaponized, too.

Used to control.

Her hair, her room, her clothes, her activities had all been controlled—micromanaged. Her mother had kept a weekly calendar on the fridge. It was adjusted every Sunday morning—but only with activities deemed important to her parents. And deviation was *not* allowed.

Quinn had learned to hide her true self. To build walls to protect that precious self. The world hurt less if she kept the well-constructed barriers in place.

She'd done what had been expected of her. It hadn't mattered that her toes screamed through another ballet practice. It hadn't mattered that she'd absorbed the cutting remarks with a smile and the criticisms without argument. Walls hadn't provided happiness, but they had kept her safe. Besides, a false smile achieved more than tears.

She'd been the docile daughter until she'd refused to let her parents control her career choices. That one rebellion had led to her being cut out of their lives—all because she'd wanted some say about her future.

But that one mutinous act had granted her freedom. The right to pick up and move to where *she* chose. To cut her hair. To dress how she wanted. To never have a planner!

And when she had her own family, they were never going to feel like their life was scheduled. Her children, if she ever settled anywhere long enough to meet someone and have children, were going to know her love didn't depend on following a plan.

"I figured I had at least another day or two." Her throat closed as she fought off tears. She never cried in front of anyone—and she wasn't going to start today. Plus, denial was easier than focusing on disaster. But Milo wouldn't understand that. He was always at least three steps ahead of everything.

It was too late to do anything about it now, though. "I'll be fine," she assured him. "You know me. If necessary, I'll find a new place." The thought of moving again made her heart sink. That was new...and not welcome.

Leaning forward, Quinn squeezed his hand. *Why was she always reaching for him?*

"Maybe somewhere that gets snow," she quipped, pulling back, "where the summers don't make me worry about melting into the pavement."

Milo's lips turned down. He'd never liked her talking about new places. He'd cheered when she'd announced that she wasn't going to work in her parents' law firm, but then he'd frowned when she'd said she was leaving California. He always frowned when she mentioned moving. She wasn't even sure he was aware he did it.

Though he hadn't frowned when she'd told him she was coming home to join him at St. Brigit's. The memory of his bright smile on that last video call still sent thrills through her.

She hated his frown—hated causing it. Her fingers itched to smooth away the small lines at the corners of his eyes. "Want to see if there's a clinic in Alaska that needs a midwife and stellar ob-gyn? We could buy some snowmobiles and race around the Arctic."

His mouth moved but no words came out. Quinn could feel the heat in her cheeks as Milo's gaze met hers. She hadn't meant to ask that and certainly hadn't expected how his stunned silence would cut across her.

"Quinn…" The question she should never have asked him hung between them as his voice died.

Concern coated Milo's features and she feared pity. That was the last thing she needed or wanted.

Especially from him.

"I'm kidding, homebody." She laughed, hoping it didn't sound as forced to him as it did to her. Maybe Milo would chalk it up to her fear and exhaustion. "I know I'll never get you out of LA. One day you're going to run the maternity ward at Valley General. I've seen the planning boards." She patted his hand.

Milo carefully managed his life. He never jumped from one contract to another. The man developed a plan. And he followed it.

No chasing a shiny, unexpected adventure.

"Enough about me." Standing, she downed the rest of her coffee. "What we should be worrying about is if those winds shift and we have to evacuate the birthing center."

"Quinn…" Milo stood and pulled her into a quick hug.

The heat from the brief connection evaporated before Quinn could blink. But the ghost of his strong arms clung to her. She wanted to step back into the embrace. She wanted to run from the room. But her feet refused to follow either order.

"It's okay to be worried about both the center and your house. I know what that tiny, falling-apart bungalow means to you."

Crossing her arms at her chest, she glared at him. "No knocking the bungalow, *Dr.* Russell. We can't all live in a fancy downtown high-rise." It was her normal retort, but her tone was sharper today. The pain of not having a home, a family, a place to belong to, stabbed her. And somehow she'd lost the ability to bury that emotion behind her walls.

"I'm sorry," Milo muttered. "That was beyond

a poor choice of words." A dimple appeared in his left cheek as he stepped up to her.

They were at work, but with the stress of the day, all Quinn wanted to do was to lose herself in Milo's arms. Let him hold her to see if that would make the stress and pain float away. They were close friends; everyone knew it. No one would raise an eyebrow if they found them embracing. But Quinn's heart wanted more.

And she wouldn't risk that.

Quinn's parents hadn't wanted her. She and her brother, Asher, hadn't talked in years. Even her ex-fiancé had found her lacking less than a month after getting down on one knee. If her relationship with Milo changed, would his need to plan everything out clash with her desire to go with her gut?

Their different approach to life worked while they were friends. But if she lost him, Quinn would be completely alone. And she couldn't stand the thought of losing the one person she'd always been able to count on.

She just couldn't.

Putting a bit of distance between them, she held up her empty coffee cup. "Thanks for the caffeine rush." Ignoring the flash of hurt that crossed Milo's features, Quinn moved for the door. He clearly didn't understand why she was being awkward, and there was no safe way for her to say *My heart's confused—sorry.*

Swallowing a pinch of panic, Quinn dropped her coffee cup into the recycle bin. As it hit the bottom, she looked over her shoulder. "I need to check on Molly."

Whatever was going on with her when she was near Milo needed to stop. They were just friends. Best friends. They'd stuck together through their awkward teen phases, all their different jobs, her failed engagement and the end of his short-lived marriage. No one knew her better. No one made her feel more grounded.

More cared for…

Her chest seized. Quinn was just lonely, longing for a place of her own. Her heart was confused. It was reaching for the comfortable. That was all.

Milo's arms were heavy as the light scent he associated with Quinn lingered in the air around him as he stared after her. She was hurting and needed a friend. Why had something that had always been so easy become such a challenge once she'd started working with him at St. Brigit's?

What if she noticed how his embraces lingered a bit too long? How he had to fight to keep from leaning his head against hers? That he longed to be near her?

It had taken over a decade for them to land in the same place at the same time. But the excitement he'd felt when she'd stepped into his arms at LAX eight months ago hadn't been grounded in friendship. He'd wanted Quinn Davis for years. He wasn't sure when the friendship they'd shared had transformed for him, but it was there in every bright smile and subtle touch. Yet she'd never indicated she wanted more. And losing her friendship wasn't an option.

He'd worked up the courage to ask her out once, years ago. But when he'd arrived with flowers, she'd been dancing with her roommate, screaming about signing her first contract with the traveling nurse agency. She'd looked so beautiful and happy. Milo had claimed "best friend telepathy" as he'd passed her the sunflowers and congratulated her on the new job.

Then he'd locked the question he'd wanted to ask deep in his heart. She had talked about putting space between her and California since elementary school. And he'd been determined to never throw a wrench into those plans. Dreams and goals were important—his father had taught him that.

Milo wanted Quinn to be happy. Wanted her to get every stamp in her passport, no matter how much he hated the distance between them...

He swallowed the desire that was his constant companion. Now wasn't the right time to ask Quinn out.

And it wasn't ever going to be right.

St. Brigit's was just a stopover for Quinn.

He knew that. Every time he sat on her lumpy, rented couch, it was a reminder that this was a landing zone after a decade on the road. And he knew the road would eventually call to her again—it always did.

It didn't call to Milo, though. He loved California and never considered relocating. His mom and his sister were in California, as were all his goals.

Still, every so often, Milo would catch a look in Quinn's eyes or a touch of a smile that made him wonder if she'd also considered exploring the possibility that there might be more between them. His brain screamed that he was imagining it, but he couldn't kill the pang of hope his heart felt each time. Last week, their hands had brushed as they'd walked to the movie theater and she'd smiled at him in a way that had Milo barely managing to prevent the words from flying out of his mouth.

These thoughts, the bloom of heat in his belly when she was near, the dreams he woke from, still feeling as though he was holding her close—he'd always been able to suppress them. But now, working with her every day, the thought that she might complete him—might patch the empty space in his soul—was growing ever stronger.

But that void had existed long before he'd met Quinn. It had been ripped open the night his father hadn't come home from the store with the supplies for his science project. His mom had done her best, but Milo had been so lonely.

The comfortable conversations he'd had with his dad hadn't been the same with his mom. He'd missed the feel of their complete family. The hole his father's passing had created still ate at him and he clung to his few memories and the emotions they stirred in him.

But if his short-lived marriage had taught him anything, it was that another person couldn't fill the void of his father's loss. That was far too much to ask. And that disaster had proved that impulsive acts just caused chaos.

And heartbreak.

Milo had always been impressed with Quinn's ability to start over. To pick up and leave the past behind when a new opportunity presented itself. She saw a new thing and ran toward it, confident that the details would sort themselves out. He let his eyes wander to the fire on the hills in the distance and sighed. But if she'd planned better, packed her car when the fire blazed closer last night… He let the thought float away.

As a kid, he'd left everything until the last minute, especially school projects. The week before he died, his dad had bought him two small whiteboards. He'd written Short Term on one and Long Term on the other—just like the headings on the boards his dad kept in his office. Then he'd explained that he wanted Milo to at least plan a few things out.

But Milo hadn't. And the night before his science presentation was due, he'd panicked because they didn't have the supplies he needed. His father had marched him upstairs and taken the money for the supplies from Milo's piggy bank, telling him he would have to do what he could but he was not to stay up past his bedtime.

While Milo had started the research, his father had gone out for supplies. A drunk driver had collided with him as he'd left the grocery store. Poster boards for Milo and flowers for his mother had been found in the car and dutifully delivered by a policeman days later.

Milo, suddenly lost, had been a mere shadow of himself. Adrift in a world where the man who'd made him feel tall, important, special, had vanished. In the grief-filled days that followed, he'd finally started using the planning boards his father had given him. The routine they'd provided had eased his pain. It never entirely vanished, but he found that rigidly structuring life left him open to fewer surprises. It gave him a bit of control in the chaotic world.

Milo was never going to be that person who had no idea what the next six months would hold. Where Quinn needed freedom, he required control. She wasn't going to stay in California, and the goals that would make him whole were set in stone.

And he was so close.

Milo made his way over to the window. Smoke had descended over LA a week ago, but the light of the fires had stayed away until now. A bead of worry moved through him as he stared at the glow just beyond the horizon. Wildfires were an all too constant threat in California and he'd experienced life with voluntary evacuation notices a few times. But he had never received a mandatory evacuation notice.

Would Quinn's house survive? He hoped so. He remembered questioning her decision to rent the rundown property when he'd helped her move her limited belongings inside almost a year ago. She'd just smiled and said she'd loved the place.

They'd spent weekends painting the gray walls of her bedroom a bright blue and her kitchen walls the color of the shining sun. If coffee didn't wake her up, the sunflower color would. Milo hadn't teased her that bright colors were out of fashion—at least according to his interior designer sister—because Quinn deserved to have walls whatever color her heart desired. He'd never understood her mother's refusal to allow Quinn to paint her childhood room, even when Quinn had offered to pay for all the supplies. But there was a lot about the Davis family that Milo hadn't understood.

The only problem Milo had with her bungalow was its distance from his place. It was forty minutes away from St. Brigit's on a good traffic day.

Forty minutes away from him…

Maybe it had been ridiculous to think she'd want to be neighbors. But he'd looked for places near him as soon as Quinn had told him she'd accepted the position at St. Brigit's. He'd plotted the best areas and done a ton of research for her. She'd signed her lease on the bungalow without ever looking at any of it. He knew she'd always trusted her gut over research, but had thought she'd want to be closer for the short time she was going to be in LA. It had hit him surprisingly hard when she'd chosen somewhere so far from him.

She'd signed a two-year lease on the two-bedroom bungalow. He should have rejoiced. But then she'd rented all her furniture. And his small piece of hope that she'd stay had died. He'd counted on having two years. But now, if the bungalow burned, would she leave again?

Even with her lease, Milo had started looking for hints that she might run off on another adventure. The nursing agency still sent her job advertisements, and he was aware that she talked to her clinic colleagues about the travel opportunities when they arose. Her excitement was contagious, and he knew at least one nurse from St. Brigit's had put in an application.

But she'd asked him to go to Alaska— No, Milo corrected his heart, Quinn had joked about finding a place somewhere else if her home turned to ashes. She'd just thrown him in—probably without thinking. After all, her cheeks had burned as soon as the question had left her lips.

He'd teased her about her tendency to blush for years and when her cheeks lit up, he'd wanted to lean forward and rub his hands over them. To pull her close.

Instead, his tongue had refused to mutter even a basic response. And then she'd confirmed that it was only a joke.

Which he'd known...

So why was his heart still wishing she'd meant it—even if he never planned to leave?

Pushing a hand through his hair, Milo tried to rope in his wayward emotions. An offhand comment when Quinn was stressed didn't mean anything.

But what if it did? What if it was a sign she wanted more from him too? The loose plan he'd thought of for asking Quinn out formed at the back of his brain again.

Why was it refusing to stay buried?

"Molly's crowning and the baby won't drop!" Rhonda shouted from behind him. She was gone before the lounge door slammed shut, giving him the perfect excuse to bury the lingering questions and thoughts, and focus on his work instead.

* * *

"I can't," Molly sighed and leaned her head back.

"You can. Just breathe. And when the next contraction comes, I need you to push with all your might." Quinn kept her voice level as Molly let out another low cry.

She'd been pushing for over an hour and was growing tired and frustrated. Quinn dropped her eyes to the baby's heart rate monitor. It was still holding steady, but the longer Molly's son refused to enter this world, the greater her chance of needing an emergency cesarean.

"I'm tired." Molly's voice ached with exhaustion.

"I know," Quinn commiserated, but only for a minute. Her nursing mentor, a former army medic, had taught each of his students that sometimes a patient needed a command. Meeting Molly's gaze, Quinn channeled her inner drill sergeant. "Your job isn't done," she reminded her. "So, Julian, help Molly sit up a bit. And Molly, get ready to bear down."

Molly's partner helped her up and rubbed her back. He whispered something in her ear, low enough that Quinn couldn't hear him. Whatever the words were, Molly set her lips and nodded at Quinn.

Good. She needed Molly focused. Bringing life into this world was hard work, but Molly could do it.

The monitor started to beep and Molly's face screwed tight. "Oh, God."

"Here we go. Push!" Quinn ordered.

Molly let out a scream as she held on to Julian's hands, but she didn't stop pushing.

And Quinn breathed a sigh. *Finally.* His little nose and lips were perfect. "Good job, Momma. One or two more pushes, and we should have him."

The air shifted next to her and Quinn knew Milo had joined them, but she didn't look up. She'd asked Rhonda to grab Milo after they'd passed the forty-minute mark of pushing. If the baby hadn't descended… Quinn swallowed. The baby had—that was all that mattered now.

Quinn was pleased that Milo's presence wasn't needed, but she knew he wouldn't leave now. Not because he didn't trust her ability to safely deliver a child, but because he cared for each of his patients. And Milo tried to be present for as many births as possible. Quinn liked to joke that he lived a block from the birthing center so that he could welcome as many little ones into this world as possible.

"Looks like I got dressed in my fancy scrubs for nothing."

Quinn could hear the smile in Milo's voice as she focused on Molly's little one. This was the part they all loved. The reason every midwife and ob-gyn entered the profession. There was no better joy than to watch new life enter this world. Sharing a few minutes with loving partners becoming first-time or fifth-time parents... It never got old.

The monitor beeping picked up and Quinn offered Molly a quick smile. "One more time, Momma."

Molly's eyes were a bit watery, but she gripped Julian's hands and pushed as the next contraction cascaded through her. "Fine!" Molly bit out. "But I am definitely telling his first date about how much trouble he put me through."

"That is every parent's right. I think it's in a handbook somewhere," Milo agreed.

Quinn laughed and then smiled as the tiny guy slid into her arms. He was perfect. Ten little toes and fingers, and a set of very healthy lungs, as evidenced by the fact he immediately erupted in a screech.

Perfect.

For just a moment, Quinn wished the child was hers. It was a need that she was having trouble ignoring lately. But it encompassed so much more. A desire to find someone. To walk through life with another, someone who'd try to keep a straight face while she crushed his hands and brought their child into this world.

Someone who would choose her, just as she was...

As she laid the still-screeching little one on

his mother's chest, Quinn grinned at her patient. "Congratulations, Molly. You're a mom—again."

Molly and Julian were good people, a loving family. Surely their hearts were big enough to include the new baby *and* their adopted son, even if he didn't share their DNA. Unlike her own parents…

The placenta was delivered with no complications as Molly and Julian bonded with their newborn—each counting his toes and fingers—before letting Milo take the baby to check him over while Quinn took care of Molly.

A few minutes later, Quinn watched as an exhausted Molly kissed the top of her son's head and then kissed her husband.

"He's beautiful," Quinn said with a smile. It was true. Their little man was adorable—like all new babies.

Molly let out a sigh. "He is. So beautiful. He looks a bit like Owen. I know technically people would say that's not possible, but look at his little nose." Molly's fingers traced a line down the boy's nose and laughed. "Such a cute nose."

Julian kissed his wife. "I agree. Though maybe that is because all baby boys seem to look like little old men when they're first born." Julian laughed and pulled out his cell phone.

A small boy appeared on the screen a few seconds later. "Am I a big brother? Am I?" Owen beamed at the baby on his mother's chest.

"Yes," Molly whispered. "This is Adam—your little brother." She let out a yawn and waved to her oldest.

Julian took over, his smile wide as he looked at Owen. "Mommy is tired, but Grandma is going to bring you to visit in a little while."

"Promise?" Owen queried.

Quinn wondered if the small boy was worried. At four, a bit of sibling jealousy was to be expected, and he was likely too young to understand that his world had altered forever. *Please...* Quinn sent out a silent prayer to the universe that it was altering for the better.

"Promise." Julian gave him a thumbs-up. "I love you, big brother."

Quinn sucked in a breath as her heart clenched. She needed to leave—now. Molly was fine, and the family needed some bonding time, anyway. She wanted to believe that was why she was ducking out. But Quinn had never been good at lying—particularly to herself.

The echoes of her past chased her as she exited the birthing room.

This wasn't her life. The reminder did little to calm her racing heart. Molly wasn't her mother and Julian wasn't her father. These parents would love both their children equally.

They would.

She'd wanted to return to California, had felt drawn here. Working with Milo had been the biggest draw, but LA was also her hometown. Where she'd been raised. She had hoped that maybe enough time had passed. But in the short time she'd been home, she'd realized the pain of her childhood refused to bury itself in the hole in her soul.

Rolling her shoulders, she tried to find a wave of calm, but it eluded her. Her parents had struggled to conceive, too. After years of trying, they'd adopted Quinn—a newborn abandoned at a fire station.

If they'd loved her then, Quinn had been too young to remember. Her brother, Asher—the miracle child they'd always wanted—had been born when she was not quite two. Overnight, Quinn had become an interloper. If they could have returned her…

Leaning against the wall, Quinn inhaled a deep breath, trying to fend off the past. Today had been too emotional. But the tiny part of her heart that wasn't happy on the road, that craved permanence, that got louder with every move… And screamed loudest when she was near Milo—

"She looks just like my mother." The soft coo of a new mom walking past with her newborn sent Quinn spiraling further.

Every time someone had commented on how her jet-black hair and dark eyes were so different from her family's blond hair and baby blues, she'd wish her mother would laugh it off. Make up a great-grandfather. Or say that she was her daughter by choice instead of by birth—other adoptive families believed that. But no matter how hard Quinn had tried to follow the family's strict rules, to abide by her parents' wants and desires, it hadn't been enough.

Instead, Carolyn Davis would calmly explain that Quinn wasn't really hers.

Not hers...not a full member of the family.

When her parents had died in a car crash right after she became a nurse, she found out that they'd left everything to her brother. She hadn't even been mentioned in the will.

Though they'd never been close, her brother had tried to make it right. Asher had divided the estate evenly. Quinn hadn't cared about the money or the real estate—her parents had stopped supporting her financially the day she'd declared that she didn't want to be a lawyer. She'd realized that that wouldn't have gained her acceptance, so why give up her dreams of being a nurse?

It wasn't his fault, but Asher had gotten the things that mattered. The letters. The keepsakes. The acknowledgment. Quinn shouldn't have expected anything. Still, part of her had hoped that one day she might be welcomed into her own family. With her parents' passing, that dream became impossible. And to not even be mentioned in the documents they'd meticulously prepared in case they died unexpectedly, was a wound she still didn't know how to mend.

Then she'd lost her brother, too. Not physically. At least, she didn't think so. But Asher had stopped returning her phone calls and picked up the reins at their parents' law firm. Their lives had always been separate, but without their parents between them, she'd hoped they might be friends, or at best, not competitors. She'd been disappointed—again.

But she'd found her place—at least professionally. Nursing was her calling and she'd never regretted choosing it. She'd carved her own path, focusing only on the step right in front of her. But nursing didn't take away her desire to be accepted, to be loved, to have a family that wanted her—just as she was.

"Molly and Julian are going to be excellent parents, and their boys are going to keep them busy." Milo's words floated over her.

"Of course they are." Quinn opened her eyes and looked toward the door where Rhonda was hanging the welcome stork. The spindle-legged creature was hung on all the doors, and Quinn's heart ached with the worry that she might never experience that joy. She was less likely to find it if she moved every year—or sooner. "I'm fine."

Maybe if she repeated the phrase, it would bloom into truth.

"I didn't ask." Milo leaned against the wall and wrapped an arm around her shoulders.

At least he hadn't directly called out her lie. Pushing away from the wall, Quinn offered him a smile, doing her best to make it seem unforced. "You were going to." She tapped her head. "Best friend telepathy."

Milo grinned. The dimple in his cheek sent a tiny thrill through her. Between working with him and hanging out with him, it was getting harder to keep the lines of friendship from blurring.

Particularly when she didn't want to.

Hurrying on before he could add any commentary, Quinn knocked a finger against her watch. "I'm off duty. So, I'm going to—" Her words died as she remembered that she couldn't go home.

"You want to crash at my place? I'm off, too."

His heat warmed the cold that refused to leave her. But if she said yes when her emotions were so close to the surface, it could be a disaster. "No." The rushed word was clipped, and her heart sank as Milo's nose scrunched.

He was worried and hurt, and there wasn't a good way to walk her tone back. She hadn't meant to hurt his feelings.

Trying to sound bright and cheery, Quinn offered, "I'll crash here, and one of the on-call midwives can have a date night!"

Someone should.

Bumping his hip, she ignored the gibe and added, "I'll certainly be on time for my next shift. Maybe even early, given the commute."

Milo nodded, but the ghost of hurt still hovered on his face. "The commute will certainly be quick."

Pursing her lips, Quinn watched him go. Longing pushed at her chest, ordered her to chase after him, to tell him she'd love to go home with him. In so many different ways…

But that was why she couldn't do it. He was her friend. If their dynamic changed, she could lose so much.

But what if she gained everything?

Until she could quash her heart's cry, she needed to keep a bit of distance between them. No matter how much it hurt.

CHAPTER TWO

QUINN'S DARK HAIR spilled across her cheeks, her breaths were slow and her feet hung from the couch. Pulling at the back of his neck, Milo sighed at the sight of the crumpled pillow she was using. He'd taken more than one nap on that monstrosity. She was going to wake with a stiff neck.

If she'd come home with him last night, she'd have been comfortable, well rested. *Cared for.* But he knew Quinn's independent side well. She'd been taking care of herself for most of her life. But she didn't have to do *every*thing herself. Relying on each other was an important part of any friendship. She could ask him for anything. Anything.

Besides, there was independence and then there was stubborn. One night on that couch was more than enough. If the evac order hadn't been lifted on her home by the end of their shift today, he was going to find a way to make her agree to stay at his place until this was over.

His heart rate picked up, and Milo wanted to slap himself. He should not be happy that she might have to stay with him.

Get hold of yourself.

Her home might be engulfed in flames at this very moment. A sobering thought...

Milo's hand shook as he reached for her shoulder, but at least she couldn't see it. "Quinn." She'd never been a quick riser. He set one alarm and never allowed it to snooze, but Quinn relied on at least three. A small smile touched her lips and she rolled toward him—as much as the couch would allow anyway. "Milo, I want..."

I want... What? He wanted to know the final part of that statement. Desperately.

She wasn't really awake. And he knew that dreams offered scattered bits of information. After all, Quinn had been a regular fixture in his dreams for years. And since her return, those dreams often woke him with decidedly less than friendly thoughts.

But that didn't mean he was a feature in her dreams. She could be dreaming of painting, cooking or any of the multitude of activities they'd done together over their two decades of friendship. Still, the small bursts of hope cutting across his heart refused to be quashed.

What if she was dreaming of more too?

He didn't have time for introspection this

morning. Gripping her shoulder, he shook harder. "Quinn."

Ainsley Dremer's husband had called to report that his wife was in labor. She'd worked out a plan for a home birth, but the midwives they'd worked with were currently dealing with mandatory evacuation orders. St. Brigit's standing rule was that two midwives attended home births, but no midwives other than Quinn were available. So, Milo was going to act as the second.

If the fire expanded, their patients might have trouble reaching St. Brigit's. He knew the first responders were doing their best, but months of drought had created the perfect landscape for the fire to grow. And grow it had.

According to the news, homes in Quinn's area had been destroyed, though he still didn't know for sure that Quinn's bungalow had been one of them. He didn't want anyone's house destroyed, but Milo especially wanted Quinn's house to stay safe. That way she wouldn't have an excuse to leave.

She belonged here…with him.

Why the hell wouldn't that thought disappear?

Warm fingers grazed his and heat rushed through Milo's body. Those little touches meant far more to him than they should. But that didn't stop him from craving them.

"Milo?" Quinn's lips turned up and her cheeks

pinkened as her eyes landed on him. "What time is it?"

"Time to get to work!" Milo winked, hoping his face didn't show the multitude of contradictory emotions floating through him. "Ainsley Dremer is in labor. Sherrie and Heather are both dealing with mandatory evac orders, so you and I are up to the plate."

Quinn flinched as she straightened and rolled her shoulders.

"This couch isn't built for long-term slumber." Milo barely resisted the urge to reach out and rub her shoulders, even though he'd performed the action dozens of times over the years—after long study sessions in college or in the weeks she'd be passing through LA before heading off to her next contract.

It was a simple gesture. One a friend could easily offer. But it felt far too intimate when his body craved so much more than just a friendly touch.

"I've slept on worse." Quinn's hand ran along her neck as she massaged the knots out. "Nothing a few pain tablets and a hot shower won't fix. Though only one of those is an option this morning."

It was her standard reply. She'd said the same thing after sleeping on the floor of a makeshift hospital in Haiti during a cholera outbreak. She'd also joked about the tiny cot she'd fallen into while living in a rural area of Maine where the roads nearly vanished in the winter. The woman seemed capable of falling asleep anywhere, but that didn't stop muscles from complaining, no matter how much she tried to hide it.

At least he was prepared this morning. Milo reached for the glass of water and passed her two pain-relief tablets. Then he held up a small bag with a toothbrush and toothpaste. Small comforts went a long way.

"Milo—" Quinn smiled "—you're the best."

The small compliment sent more than a few shivers down his spine. She was being Quinn. His wonderful, amazing, best friend. But it wasn't enough.

Hadn't been enough for years.

"The service here is going to be hard for my next locale to live up to." Tipping the water bottle toward him, she grinned. "To friends."

"Friends," Milo repeated, bitterness coating his tongue.

Her "next locale." Such a simple phrase. *An expected phrase.* This was just a waypoint. And he needed to remember that.

He tried to force his voice to sound normal. "I am pretty amazing." Milo wished he had more caffeine in his system.

"And so humble." Quinn laughed as she set the water bottle down and grabbed the bag of toiletries. "How far along is Ainsley? Sherrie was her primary. Thankfully, she said Ainsley's pregnancy was textbook."

Home births were rising in popularity in the US, and Milo fully supported them. But he did not recommend them for women with possible birthing risks. Milo loved that St. Brigit's offered both options for his patients. Just like his mother's clinic did.

His heart compressed a tiny bit. He hadn't worked at that clinic in nearly five years. St. Brigit's was great, but it wasn't Oceanside Clinic.

No place was.

And five years ago, when his mother had married Felix Ireman, another ob-gyn at the clinic, the place had taken on an even more homey feel. Milo'd spent most of his teen years volunteering at Oceanside and, during his undergrad years, had even sketched out an idea to add a natural birthing center, which they'd started building the year he'd worked there.

Oceanside Clinic was special and he'd only experienced the feeling he got when he stepped into Oceanside at one other place. Valley General.

Three weeks before his father had passed, he'd had a meeting at Valley General. He'd taken Milo along so he could interview a surgeon for a science project. The one Milo had put off.

As they were leaving, his father had slowed next to the chief of obstetrics' office. He'd smiled at Milo and said, "One day, this will be my office." The memory of the confidence in his father's voice still caused goose pimples to rise on Milo's skin.

It was the clearest memory he had of his dad. His father's voice might have been lost to the waste bin of memory, but that day, that perfect day and all its feelings, Milo remembered. His dad had never achieved that goal—but Milo would. And each morning, when he walked through the door, he'd feel close to his dad again.

"Milo?"

Ignoring the ache in his chest, Milo focused on Quinn's original question. "She is forty weeks and two days. When her husband called, the contractions had been holding steady since a little after three. So it's showtime!"

Milo glanced at the window. The sun wouldn't rise for another two hours, but the glow of orange still lit up the hills in the distance. "Ainsley and her husband are a few miles from the voluntary evacuation zone."

Quinn's eyes hovered on the hills through the window. "Did the winds shift overnight?" Her lips tipped down before she shook herself. "I meant…are they expecting them to shift? Morning brain."

The attempt to cover her worry didn't fool him. Of course she was wondering if her home had survived the night. And he didn't have an answer for her. But rather than pull on the first thread, he addressed her second question. "Have to ask someone more versed in fire control than me." He knew the department's director was in regular contact with the city fire brigades and that conditions had been deemed safe enough for them to head out.

Quinn moved toward the bathroom. "Give me five minutes to take care of necessities, and then we'll be on our way." Before she closed the door, Quinn added, "And don't eat all the croissants. I saw the bag behind your back."

Milo laughed. "I make no promises."

Their director opened the door to the employee lounge just then. "Dr. Russell, if the fire shifts and there are complications with Ainsley Dremer's delivery, I've instructed Kevin to run you south to Oceanside Clinic."

The bag nearly slipped from Milo's hands as he tried to steady the beat of his heart. *Oceanside*. Did they really expect the fire to shift? And if so, why were they not directing Ainsley and her husband to either head to St. Brigit's now or to go south to Oceanside? Plans and routes ran through Milo's head.

"Dr. Russell?" Martina stepped into the room, lines crossing her forehead.

She met his gaze then let her eyes wander to the window. "They aren't anticipating the fire shifting. We would never risk anyone's safety. But it's always good to have a backup plan."

"Of course," Milo agreed. Plans were how he lived his life. He just hated the small bead of want that always pressed against his soul when he thought of the Oceanside Clinic. He'd loved working with his mom, but with each passing year, his connection to his father slipped farther away, making him more determined to get the job at Valley General. For a kid that had been his dad's shadow—to not even remember his dad's voice...

Pain rippled down his neck as he tried to recall it, but it refused to materialize. Valley General offered Milo an opportunity no other place would. If he could reestablish that connection to that last blissful day they'd shared, then maybe the loneliness he hadn't fully conquered since would dissipate.

It might vanish completely if Quinn stayed. Suddenly his body was on fire for a different reason. He couldn't go down this path. She'd mentioned her "next locale" less than fifteen minutes ago.

"Didn't realize we would need to go that far south. Caught me by surprise. That's all."

Martina nodded. "Ainsley and her husband are halfway between here and Oceanside. Easier to head south from there. You know how it is. No one can afford the city rents. And since you still have visiting rights at Oceanside, it makes the most sense."

He'd maintained his position as a visiting physician at his mother's clinic, but only in the event of an emergency or if his mother and Felix were unable to work. Thankfully, that had never happened. Though, if his mother kept talking about him coming back, he might need to end it. She knew what Oceanside meant to Milo, and she also knew about his dreams for Valley General. "Glad it's finally come in handy." Milo lifted his cup of coffee. "Quinn and I will be ready to go soon. Is there anything else you need from us? We'll probably be with Ainsley for most of the day."

"Since you asked… Dr. Metri is looking over a few résumés for the open OBG position. When you get back, I'd like you to look them over, too. See if there is anyone you think would make a good addition to our team. There's even one from a senior Valley General ob-gyn. Guess she's looking to slow down a bit."

Valley General. An open senior position.

His tongue stuck to the roof of his mouth as he glanced toward the door where Quinn was getting ready. Working with Quinn was one of the top highlights of his career. He'd assumed she'd be the first to leave, but could he leave before her?

Mercy General had approached him a few weeks ago about a potential senior OB position. The opportunity would've enhanced his résumé for any potential opening at Valley General, but he'd passed. His credentials were already impressive, and Quinn might never make it back to California once she left. Their working relationship had an expiration date, even if neither of them discussed it, and he just wasn't willing to cut things short.

Valley General! his brain screamed. *It's only ten miles up the road.* But his heart was less willing to celebrate the potential coup. Still, he could look at the résumés.

"Of course." Milo nodded and smiled as Martina walked out. If a senior OB was looking to leave Valley General, perhaps he could accelerate his plan. It would make Quinn's transition back to the road easier to accept.

Maybe keep him from making a fool of himself, too.

"What's up?" Quinn asked as she grabbed the white bag from Milo's fingers. "You look like you're planning something."

"How can you tell?" Milo grabbed a croissant from the bag.

She hit his hip with hers as she raised the pastry to her lips. "The far-off look and rubbing your chin. It's cartoonish but adorable."

She'd been able to read him like that since they'd been teenagers. It was comforting, but what if she saw the swirls of emotion directed at her? Milo's throat tightened as he purposely removed his hand from his chin. "I see."

Quinn's fingers burned as she gripped his wrist. "It really is a cute trait. So, what are you planning?"

"Nothing major." Milo started for the door. "Martina wants me to look over a few résumés. Apparently, one of them is from a senior OB at Valley General."

Quinn fell into step beside him. She was tearing off pieces of her pastry, but her eyes had a faraway look in them. "So, you're plotting how to become their replacement at Valley General?"

"It's not plotting." Milo sighed and hated the flash of hurt that hovered in Quinn's eyes before she strode past him.

Following her to the van bay, Milo opened the back door as their driver, Kevin, started the engine. "I'm sorry. But 'plotting' sounds so much more sinister than 'planning,' which is what I always do. Stay the course." He chuckled, but it sounded false, even to him.

Quinn nodded as she finished her croissant. "Plans can shift. You're the only one writing them in stone."

"What is that supposed to mean?" Milo's stomach hollowed as her gaze met his. Their ability to read each other could really be a curse.

"Milo." Quinn raised a brow. "Ever since Bianca left, Valley General has become your obsession." She leaned her head against the wall of the medical van as it turned out of the parking lot.

"Planning is not an obsession. It gives you control." Milo frowned as Quinn's dark gaze held his.

"Control doesn't—" Quinn bit her lip so hard he feared she was tasting blood, but she didn't continue the well-worn argument.

Quinn moved with her heart; she didn't look for stepping stones in her career. And she didn't understand why he was so focused on Valley General when St. Brigit's and Oceanside had made him happy, too.

He'd been lost after Bianca's infidelity less than six months into their impulsive Vegas marriage. It had been ridiculously cliché and completely out of character, but when Bianca had said it would be nice for them to be bound to each other forever, it had called to the lonely place inside him.

They'd been together for almost a year at that point, and he'd considered proposing, but the time hadn't ever seemed right. Still, he'd rationalized that they'd have done it eventually, so he'd said yes and they'd walked down the aisle.

And in the end, not waiting, not planning, had cost him. He might not be able to remember his father clearly, but the image of his ex in bed with another man was certainly seared into his brain.

He'd stepped off the path he'd outlined and chaos had erupted. In less than a year, he'd gone from married doctor to the source of gossip, particularly when Bianca had announced her pregnancy less than three months after she'd left him.

Luckily, his mother had offered him a position at Oceanside. He'd spent a year there regrouping, and the memory of his father at Valley General, and how right everything had felt in that moment, had begun to consume him. He needed to make it a reality. *He did.*

Quinn kept her eyes closed, but he could see the twitch of her lips. She wanted to say something, probably wanted to run through the pros of letting his heart lead. But it was. It was leading him to Valley General.

It was ironic for a traveling nurse to seem so invested in him staying in one place, something he'd kidded her about a few times. She liked to say that it would be nice if one of them settled down.

Why couldn't it be her?

Ainsley and her husband, Leo, met Quinn and Milo at the door with forced smiles. "Who would have thought we'd be bringing a babe into the world as it burns?" the mom-to-be quipped nervously.

"Well, this isn't California's first drought. We'll be fine. I'm sure," Leo said, kissing Ainsley's head, his gaze not leaving the smoke that was much heavier than even Quinn thought it should be.

They'd checked as they'd driven, and the voluntary evacuation zone was less than fifteen miles north of Ainsley and Leo's neighborhood. Unless luck shifted for the firefighters, this area was going to be under voluntary evacuation orders eventually. Quinn hadn't known much luck in her life, but maybe today...

Ainsley gripped her belly with one hand and the doorknob with the other.

"Breathe," Milo offered as he stepped up beside Quinn.

"I...know." Ainsley's eyes were firmly shut as she forced the words out. When the contraction loosened, she met their gazes and stepped aside. "Sorry. Welcome to our home."

"It's not a problem." Quinn smiled as she gripped the strap of her midwifery bag and stepped across the threshold. A birthing pool was ready in the center of the living room, and a pile of towels lay next to it. But it was the stack of boxes sitting next to the front door that caught Quinn's eye.

"I thought it might be good to put a few things together...if..." Leo's words were soft as he looked from Quinn to the boxes. "It's mostly baby stuff and paperwork. I've almost put them in the car a dozen times today. Every time I start,

I think I'm tempting fate if I do, then worry that I'm tempting it by not. Crazy thoughts while my wife is giving birth, right?"

Quinn understood Leo's rambling logic. She offered the expectant father a smile. "I think you should go ahead and pack it." There was little that a partner could control during a birth. Quinn had seen more than one spouse spiral as they tried to find something to do to help.

And she couldn't push away the bubble of fear in her mind that wanted to scream at her for not doing the same. Her boxes may have turned to ash, but Leo and Ainsley's were still whole.

When Leo hesitated, Quinn added, "You can always take them out later. But if you don't do it, you're just going to keep worrying. And Ainsley will need all your focus soon."

Leo stared at the boxes for a moment longer before looking down the hallway to where Ainsley was pacing. Then his eyes moved to the center of the living room where Milo was pulling supplies from his medical bag. "You're right. Can't hurt."

Moving toward Milo, Quinn set her midwifery bag next to his. The supplies in one kit should be enough, but each practitioner carried their own bag when they went to home deliveries.

"Nice job. Having those boxes in the car will relax Leo a bit." Milo's voice was low as he checked the oxygen and syringes from his bag.

Every person she'd worked with had an item or two that was always triple-checked. For Milo, it was oxygen and syringes. For her, it was the maternal and infant resuscitators—items she always prayed would stay packed. "You have a gift for finding the right words."

"Thanks." Quinn nodded. The tiny compliment was nice, but did little to fill the hollow in her stomach that just wanted to know if she still had boxes. If the few precious items she loved were intact.

"It'll be okay." Milo's voice was soft as he kept an eye focused on Ainsley as she paced the hallway.

"What if it isn't? What if everything is gone?" She wanted to kick herself, but there was no way to reel the words back in. Now was not the time or the place.

"Then we buy new things." Milo looked at the oxygen tank for the third time. "And make new memories together. Like helping bring a baby into the world while a fire rages on the doorstep."

Together. Such an easy word with so much meaning. How did he always manage to find the right words? A calmness pressed through her as she stared at him. Milo always put people at ease. It made him a wonderful friend and a great doctor. How many people would have thought to bring water and pain tablets to make the start of her day easier?

But it was more for her. Quinn knew that. Milo grounded her. He was her point of reference. The haven she knew she could come home to anytime, but also the one who would always cheer her on as she found her next adventure.

She wished there was an easy way to return the favor. She might not understand his connection to his father, but she could see how important it was to him. Yet she was terrified he wasn't living his life, not really.

How could he when he was so focused on a memory?

But maybe her desire to run from nearly everything about her past was what fogged her brain— Right now wasn't the time to focus on that. When her mind was more at ease, and less prone to jumping to inopportune thoughts about her best friend, Quinn would find a way to at least mention the cons of running a large unit like the one at Valley General.

He'd miss things like home deliveries and spending extra time with patients—and Quinn didn't think that would make Milo happy.

Was a memory enough to carry him through? Was it worth it?

"I'm going to go wash up and see how far along Ainsley is." Quinn tapped Milo's shoulder as she grabbed her box of gloves and headed for the kitchen. Her fingers tingled from the brief contact, but she ignored that feeling as Ainsley came to stand beside her.

"How far apart are the contractions?"

"About four minutes." Ainsley's face contorted a bit as she gripped the edge of the counter. "Nope, three and a half."

Quinn held out her arms and gestured for Ainsley to grip her forearms as she breathed through the contraction. "Three and a half minutes is good. Breathe. As soon as this one ends, let's see how far along you are. Then, if you want to get into the birthing pool, now would probably be a good time."

"Okay," Ainsley whispered as she released her grip on Quinn's forearms. She looked at the pool and let out a sigh as they walked toward her bedroom. "I planned to spend most of my labor there. But when it started, walking felt better. Leo spent so much time setting it up for me."

"Labor often throws plans out the window." Milo's grin was brilliant as he joined them in the hall.

Quinn shot him a quick look as she followed Ainsley into the bedroom. He was quite willing to grant everyone else the grace to change their plans. Shame he couldn't offer the same grace to himself.

"Dr. Russell is right. If you want to keep walking, that is fine. Leo will understand." Quinn kept her voice level as Ainsley slid onto the bed, which had been prepared with medical-grade covers and protective layers. Many mothers planned out their home births for months. And they became very attached to specific ideas that might have to be adjusted or just weren't what they wanted during labor. There was no shame in changing plans, though.

"I hope so." Ainsley lay back and gripped her belly as another labor pain started.

That one hadn't taken three minutes. "Milo!" Quinn called.

"This…one…is…bad!" Ainsley's face contorted.

She was likely moving into transition labor. There was going to be a little one here shortly.

Milo stepped to the door and took in the scene before him. "I'll get the bags."

As the contraction ended, Quinn checked Ainsley. "Nine centimeters. It won't be long now. I think we need to just stay here and not worry about the tub."

"Here…works." Ainsley shook her head as another contraction started. "Leo?"

Milo returned, dropping the bags next to the bed. "I'll go grab him."

Before Milo could leave, Leo stepped into the room with a police officer.

Quinn felt her heart drop. Milo caught her gaze and she saw fear in his eyes too, though he didn't adjust his position. If the officer was here, the winds must have shifted again. Luck really wasn't on their side, but Milo clearly wasn't going to panic.

"See, we can't leave." Leo's whisper wasn't low enough.

Milo's face paled, but he moved quickly. "I'll go get the stretcher and Kevin." Milo nodded to the officer as he darted from the room.

"No." Ainsley's lip quivered. "Please…"

"Sorry, ma'am." The officer nodded. "But the fire is moving faster than expected. This area is under mandatory evacuation and you need to leave. *Now!*" He tipped his head toward Leo. "I need to see to the rest of the neighborhood."

"Leo." Quinn kept her tone firm as she looked between Leo and Ainsley. "We are headed to Oceanside Clinic. Meet us there."

"I can't leave my wife." Leo's cheeks were red and tears coated his eyes.

"We do not have room for you in the van. Dr. Russell and I need to focus on your wife. Plus, you need to get those boxes to safety." Quinn was surprised her voice was so steady, but she was grateful.

Adrenaline was coursing through her. She'd been in several crisis situations—though never this close to home.

And never fire.

At least it was Milo here with her now. They worked seamlessly as a team, and this delivery was going to be difficult just because of the circumstances. If anyone could handle delivering a baby while on the run from a wildfire, it was Milo.

"I need you to go, so I can take care of your wife and baby." Quinn walked over to Leo but didn't touch him with her gloved hands. She needed to remain sterile. "Ainsley needs all our focus, and she needs to know that you are safe and will be there to meet her at Oceanside."

"Give me a kiss and then go!" Ainsley said, her voice strong despite the tears slipping across her cheeks.

Leo shuddered, but he walked to his wife and dropped a kiss on her forehead. "Race you south, sweetheart."

"I'm right behind you." Ainsley's hands were shaking.

Quinn knew she was trying to hide the contraction. If Leo knew how much pain she was in, how close their child was to this world, he'd never leave. She glanced at her watch—less than a minute since the last one. Transition labor was the shortest phase, and she wished Ainsley had spent just a bit more time in it.

Ainsley laid her head back as Leo left. "I have to push."

No! Quinn rechecked Ainsley, and fear skittered across her skin. They needed to move her. But Ainsley was right, the baby was crowning.

"We need to move." Milo's voice was controlled as he pulled the stretcher into the room. His nose was scrunched tight.

How close is the fire?

"She's crowning. How much time do we have?" Quinn asked, then looked back at Ainsley. "I need you to do your best not to push for me. Don't hold your breath," she added as crimson traveled across Ainsley's cheeks. "Pretend that you are blowing out a candle."

It was a trick Quinn had learned in Puerto Rico during a category four hurricane. They'd had to deliver patients in near darkness with the howling wind pulling at the roof. She'd used it a few times to slow quick labor since, though never in such dire circumstances. She didn't like having to use it during a crisis again.

"All the time we need." Milo smiled, but Quinn saw his jaw clench as he maneuvered the stretcher closer. He was lying.

Dear God.

Her lungs heavy, Quinn forced herself to breathe evenly. They needed to get Ainsley, her baby and themselves to safety. "Okay."

Milo gripped Quinn's arm and looked at her gloved hands. Lowering his voice, he motioned to the stretcher. "I'm not gloved. If I move her, are you okay to handle delivery?"

"Of course," Quinn stated. "But we could stay until she delivers. It won't be…"

Milo's gaze softened, though he barely shook his head.

"Dear… God…" Ainsley muttered. "I need to push."

"Breathe for me until it passes." Quinn held her finger up, mimicking a candle, and breathed with her. Everyone needed to be calm for what was coming next. This trick worked around sixty percent of the time in Quinn's experience. The longer they waited…

As the contraction receded, Quinn let out a soft sigh. If they were going to move her, it had to be now. "Dr. Russell is going to get you onto the stretcher. Then you can push. I promise," Quinn reassured her. Ainsley nodded, but Quinn could see the fear dancing across her features. Her birth plan had just gone up in smoke, and the disaster that had seemed a bit distant was now on their doorstep.

"All right, Ainsley." Milo's voice was low and steady as he slipped an arm under her shoulders. "Wrap your arms around my neck—just like you see in the movies."

Ainsley let out a tight laugh and did as Milo instructed. "At least I'll have a story to tell this little one."

"She'll love hearing about it, I'm sure. At least until she's a teenager." Milo winked as he put his other arm under Ainsley's knees and lifted her quickly. He wasn't even breathing deeply.

Quinn had seen him work through difficult deliveries—always focused on his patient—but this delivery was one of a kind…she hoped. During her travels, she had witnessed more than one medical professional stumble when the world seemed intent on putting every obstacle in the way. But Milo was in complete control.

As he clicked the emergency belt into place, Ainsley let out another ragged breath and lifted her knees. "I can't stop—"

Quinn understood. Eventually, the body refused to delay the birthing process. At least she was on the stretcher. "Give me a push then. Just don't use all your force. We're saving that for the van."

"I wish… Leo…was here," Ainsley muttered.

"He'll meet us at the…" Quinn's voice dropped away as they stepped out the front door. The orange glow was just over the hill.

Dear God…

"The smoke…" Ainsley coughed as Milo raced them toward the van.

Wrenching the doors open, Milo lifted the stretcher and motioned for Quinn to get in. "Let's roll, Kevin!" Milo's voice cracked as the first bit of strain broke through his composure.

The doors slammed shut, and Quinn repositioned herself to be able to take care of Ainsley. The van started moving, and Quinn braced her feet against the doors the way they'd been trained to do in an emergency situation.

She'd been through a few instances where a home birth became critical and they'd had to transport the mother to the hospital. But the world hadn't been engulfed in flames then. Quinn took a deep breath as the world now dimmed to just her, Ainsley and Milo. She couldn't control anything about the fire.

The van's siren echoed through to the back, and Quinn met her patient's gaze. "Okay, Ainsley. Time to go to work."

In no time, Quinn was holding a beautiful, perfect and very angry baby girl. As her screams erupted in the van, Quinn smiled and laid the baby on Ainsley's chest. "Good job."

She finally let herself start to relax as Milo cleaned the baby as much as was possible given the circumstances. The baby was here and safe. Ainsley's delivery had been textbook—minus the evacuation.

Everything was fine…

As soon as that happy thought exited Quinn's mind, Kevin slammed on the breaks. Quinn lost her footing. She tried to grab herself, but the edge of the gurney connected with the side of her temple.

Pain erupted up her arms as her knees and palms connected with the floor of the van. "Oh!"

Quinn blinked, trying to force the black dots dancing in her eyes away.

"Quinn!" Milo's fingers were warm and soft against her forehead as he reached for her. "Hell, Kevin!"

"Sorry!" Kevin shouted as he threw the van into Reverse. "A tree limb fell across the street. Hold on!"

"Is she all right?" Ainsley's voice was taut as the tires squealed again.

"She's going to be fine," Milo said with more certainty than he felt. The cut above Quinn's eye was bleeding, but her pupils were focused. He wasn't sure what the world outside looked like, but he *was* certain he didn't want to know given Kevin's muttered curses.

"Of course I am." Quinn's smile didn't quite reach her eyes, and Milo was stunned when she offered Ainsley a thumbs-up before grabbing gauze and pressing it against the wound. This was the woman who ran into crisis situations, who was comfortable—or at least didn't mind— small cots in areas damaged by natural disasters or ravaged by disease.

He'd seen her in action at St. Brigit's, but the true core of strength running through Quinn hadn't been visible until now. No wonder her nursing agency still sent her open positions, and the contacts she'd made while serving with

Doctors Without Borders regularly called or texted her.

"How bad is it?" Quinn leaned forward, "Give it to me straight, Doctor." *And* she was trying to put him and Ainsley at ease, even as blood dripped from the bandage she was holding.

The side of his lip tipped up as he pushed a strand of her dark hair back. She was something else.

"The cut is going to need stitches, but it could have been worse." Milo swallowed as he grabbed another sterile pad and pressed it over the one that was against her forehead. If she'd fallen differently or if the van had hit the tree Kevin had swerved to miss…

Focus on the now!

Milo leaned back and sighed. "Well, this has been quite the day."

"Nothing preps you for running from a wildfire." Ainsley kissed the top of her baby's head and pushed a tear away.

"Nope." Quinn's voice was steady. "But I've served in several crisis zones, and it helps to focus on what you can control. And you did beautifully, Ainsley."

"My heart refuses to stop pounding." Ainsley let out a nervous chuckle. "You and Dr. Russell make this look easy."

"I am just following Quinn's lead. This is, fortunately, my first time running from a crisis."

Milo offered a playful salute, hoping he came off as collected as Quinn.

"But he's fantastic in all situations. There were multiple times when I was with Doctors Without Borders when I wished Milo had been there to help stabilize a tense situation." Quinn grinned as she pressed another gauze pad to her forehead. "And apparently head injuries make me talkative. So, Momma, what's her name?"

Milo tried to focus on the conversation floating between the women as the van raced south, but he kept coming back to Quinn's words. Had she really wished for him to be with her while she'd been working with the humanitarian medical group?

Or was she just trying to project calm in this rapidly changing situation? And why did the idea of serving in such a manner send a thrill through him?

Milo sucked in a breath and ignored the subtle glance Quinn gave him. They needed to get Ainsley checked in at Oceanside, and then to figure out their next steps. And those steps involved getting back to LA, with the fire blocking multiple routes, not addressing the unwelcome desire to follow up with Quinn on her statement.

CHAPTER THREE

"It's a good thing you kept your town house in Oceanside," Quinn said, leaning against Milo's shoulder as he put the key in the lock. They smelled of smoke, and it had taken them nearly twice as long as it should have to reach Oceanside. Then Milo had insisted that she let him check the cut on her forehead after they'd gotten Ainsley and her daughter checked into the Clinic and said a brief hello to Milo's stepdad, Felix.

Now she had six stitches above her eye, and she couldn't remember the last time she'd been this exhausted. She'd been in tense situations multiple times during her career, though, so Quinn knew from experience that her brain was too wired to let her drift into oblivion.

Her stomach growled—another function the body forgot about during stress.

When had they last eaten?

"Tell me you have food in the fridge!"

"Nope." Milo swung the door open. "It's fully furnished, since I rent it out most weekends as a vacation spot. But the rent doesn't include food. Luckily, it's not due to be occupied for the rest of the month. Wildfire concern caused my last two renters to back out."

Her stomach roiled with emptiness, but she ignored it. Focusing on her hunger wouldn't make food magically appear. "At least I can get a hot shower," Quinn sighed.

"And our Thai food should be here by the time you're done. I ordered it while you were saying hi to Felix."

"You are the best!" Quinn wrapped her arms around his neck without thinking. Today had been hell, even though it had ended well on all fronts. She didn't care that they were both starving and in desperate need of showers. She just wanted to hold him, to remind herself that they were fine. Her body molded to his as Milo's strong arms pulled her closer.

Her day's fears melted as he held her. This was where she wanted to be *so badly*. Her fingers itched to run through his short hair. To trace her lips along the edge of his jaw and see what happened. Sparks flew across her back as his fingers tightened on her waist.

If she held him any longer... Quinn swallowed. This embrace had already gone on for too long. She needed to stop this before Milo started to think she was crazy.

Her cheeks were warm as she pulled away. "I promise not to steal all the hot water."

"Wait." Milo grabbed her hand.

Her body vibrated with need as Milo ran his fingers along the bandage on her forehead. His touch burned as she stared at his lips.

So close, and yet so far away.

"The bandage I put on seems watertight." Milo's husky tone raced around her.

"Since you put it on less than an hour ago, I would hope so."

Was he looking for reasons to touch her?

"Yes, but it's important the wound doesn't get wet." His words were so matter-of-fact.

Of course they were.

He was a good physician and her oldest friend.

But just for a moment, she'd thought he might need to touch her, need to be near her, to hold her, too.

"I should clean up." Her throat was dry as she pulled away, but Milo didn't stop her again.

When humans were stressed or escaped catastrophe, they often sought comfort in the arms of another. A reminder that they'd lived to fight another day. She'd seen it happen when she was serving in areas that had been hit by earthquakes and floods. It was standard. But Quinn had never felt the urge to seek out that comfort—until tonight.

Until Milo...

Milo cleared his throat as he started to follow her. "There should still be some of Bianca's old clothes in the back closet. They got left behind when we separated, and she never picked them up. I'll see if I can find something you can wear."

Bianca… That name sent a cold splash down Quinn's spine. Quinn had never gotten along with the woman. She'd tried, but Bianca always seemed cold to her—unwelcoming. But she'd been Milo's choice, so Quinn had kept her mouth shut.

When he'd called to tell her that they had gotten married in Vegas, she'd cried for almost a week. For a man who planned everything, she'd been stunned that Milo had run off with Bianca for the weekend—even if they were overdue for a vacation after their residencies—and to get married on a whim?

Quinn had also been hurt that he hadn't at least told her beforehand. She'd have video-called to support him. Even if she'd thought Bianca hadn't been worthy.

She'd been right about that and hated the small part of her that had been happy when Milo had told her it was over. He'd been hurt—and happy shouldn't have been an emotion she'd felt. But maybe a small part of her had wanted him even then. Quinn was certainly not going to examine that thought tonight.

Milo was the best part of her life. He had deep

roots in this state, and he deserved someone who would walk beside him as he followed his plans.

Someone who supported him.

And Bianca had not been Milo's match even before she'd cheated on him.

Quinn's throat closed at the realization that she wasn't his match, either. Her parents had ensured she'd known exactly where her faults lay. Too flighty. Too needy. Impulsive. She led with her heart. She'd always support Milo's dreams, but checking off items on a list, trying to control everything? That wasn't something Quinn could do.

She should be happy just being best friends with Milo. Her heart skipped around him, but she could put it back in its place. Maybe returning to California had been a mistake. But she'd felt called here. Like she needed to come home—at least for a little while.

It was a feeling she still couldn't explain, but Quinn had always chosen new locations and jobs by what felt right. And working with Milo had felt right—still felt right.

So why was it so hard?

Turning on the shower, Quinn quickly stripped off her scrubs and tried to push away the thoughts of the man just outside the door.

How does Milo kiss?

She shivered despite the heat of the water.

"Quinn?" Milo's voice raced across her and

goose pimples rose on her skin. "Can I put the clothes on the counter?"

"Yes." Her tongue felt thick, but she forced the word out.

"Quinn?" Milo's voice echoed in the small bathroom, and Quinn held her breath. What was he going to say?

Part of her brain screamed to be bold. To stick her head around the curtain and suggest they conserve water. But that was just the craziness of the day talking.

Quinn had never been bold in her relationships. She always looked for the reasons why they would fail. Even when James had proposed, she'd wondered when her world would upend... though she'd expected it would be longer than three weeks.

Her guard had been up ever since.

No matter how often she told her brain to stop, it always tried to identify any signs that a partner was getting ready to leave her.

When would they throw her out of their life?

If her parents could discard her so easily, then anyone could.

She'd become an expert in identifying the subtle shifts in people. Noticed the moment the nurse she'd met in Puerto Rico discussed moving and asked her opinion as an afterthought. Her brain had tweaked the first time the oil manager she'd dated in Alaska canceled a date and mentioned his full schedule. So Quinn had ended the relationships. Better to leave first.

If you left first, the hurt wasn't as deep. Her family had drilled that lesson into her. But that did not lend itself to sultry risk-taking.

When he didn't say anything, Quinn worked up her courage. "Still out there?"

"Food is here." Milo's husky voice drifted over the curtain, an emotion she couldn't place deep within it.

Quinn wondered if he'd wanted to say something else.

Get it together!

"Remember, you promised not to use all the hot water," Milo joked.

"Well, I'd be done faster if you'd take your leave." She heard him chuckle and forced her shoulders to relax. They were both exhausted from the day, burning through the last reserves of their adrenaline. After they'd showered and had food, their bodies would sleep for the next ten hours.

Focus. Stop letting adrenaline control your hormones.

She raced through the rest of her shower and quickly dried off. Pulling on the shorts he'd left on the counter, Quinn's heart raced as she held up the green tank top. It had a built-in shelf bra, which meant that she wouldn't have to put on her smoke-scented bra, but it was a much lower cut than she usually wore.

It would have looked great on Bianca. She'd had full breasts and a curvy frame. On Quinn's athletic figure, it was much more likely to highlight her lack of assets. She sighed as she pulled it on.

Then she began to remove the bandage on her forehead. Stitches needed to be kept dry and uncovered for the first forty-eight hours, but she'd needed to shower to wash away the day's grime and smoky residue.

Between the dark circles under her eyes, the wet hair, the borrowed clothes and the cut, Quinn looked less than desirable.

Which was fine.

But she also felt downright pathetic. Were the borrowed outfit and the smoky scrubs the only things she had to her name?

"I'm going to eat all the pad thai if you keep hogging the bathroom!" Milo called out.

The ghost of a smile pulled at her lips. She'd told Milo that she'd had nothing when her parents had disowned her following her admittance to UCLA's school of nursing. He'd put his hand in her hand and said, "Nope. You have me."

"You better not!" Whatever tomorrow brought, she could handle it. As long as she had her friend by her side.

Milo's gaze fell on her as she stepped up to the

kitchen counter. Heat tore across Quinn's skin, but she refused to acknowledge it. "I will not apologize for eating all the food if you're just going to stare at me. I know I look like I need a belly full of food, followed by ten hours of sleep."

"You always look perfect." Milo grinned. "Or at least presentable."

Presentable... That was a word.

"Well, hop into that shower so we can dig in." Picking up one of the boxes, she nodded in the direction of the bathroom.

Why was he just standing there? Did she look that bad?

"Go shower, Milo. I promise there will be enough here for you to have dinner."

"I'm counting on you to share." He paused right in front of her.

His face was so close. What would he do if she lifted her head and kissed him? Just as Quinn started to follow through, Milo stepped back.

"I plan on taking the quickest shower ever!" Milo raced down the small hallway.

Quinn let out a breath as she stared at his retreating form. His smoky scent still clung to her senses. Grabbing plates from the cabinet, she began to set their dinner out. Anything to try to keep her mind from wandering to thoughts of how he might kiss.

The shower shut off in record time, and Quinn

jumped. She could do this. It was just Milo. Except there was nothing *just* about Milo. At least, not anymore.

Presentable. He'd called her presentable!

What the hell, Milo?

Perfect, wonderful, sexy—all of those were descriptions for Quinn. *Never* presentable.

He wanted—needed—to get back to her. Today had been an emotional roller coaster. When he'd watched her fall, his heart had stopped. It had only been a minor cut, but his need to hold her, no matter how unprofessional, had been overwhelming. He'd barely managed to keep it together.

He needed a plan. Plans gave him peace, a sense of order—control. He could follow a plan. Quinn was at St. Brigit's for at least another few months. Maybe she'd stay if he asked her to. Was that what he wanted?

Yes!

True, she loved being a traveling nurse and working around the world. But life was here. Could he ask her to give that up? *Sure.* But should he? Maybe not. Yet suddenly he wasn't sure that he cared.

As that selfish thought rolled through him, Milo promised himself he'd find a way to broach the topic. Not tonight. Their day had been too hectic. Their emotions were still packed too tightly with adrenaline and fear to really know what they wanted. And even if he did know, Milo needed to sort out the best way to approach all of this.

Coward! his brain shouted as he toweled his short hair dry. His heart knew what he wanted.

But Quinn always left. She chased adventure and never stayed in one place for too long. What if they started dating and a new job—a better job—materialized half a world away?

Could he handle losing her?

He shivered as the silence of the town house registered. They were all alone. That wasn't new—yet the lack of distractions felt dangerous. His stomach skittered.

It was just him and Quinn. His tongue was tied around her, and his body wanted to act. When she'd walked out in that low-cut green tank top, Milo had ached to pull her to him. His fingers had pulsed with the need to run along her sides. He'd had to grip the side of the kitchen counter just to keep from rushing toward her.

How could he address these racing thoughts with Quinn?

No immediate answer came to Milo as he dropped a shirt over his head. He would think better after dinner and some sleep. Maybe tomorrow? No. He wouldn't rush this. It was Quinn. So the plan—if he used it—had to be perfect.

"Did you eat it all?" Milo picked up an empty

container on the counter. Then he froze. The table was set and Quinn was pouring wine. The shorts he'd grabbed for her hugged her derriere and highlighted her long, slim legs. His mouth watered as he imagined trailing kisses up her thighs. "I figured we'd just eat out of the paper cartons."

Quinn's dark eyes met his and her lips pulled up into a smile. "We spent the day outrunning a fire while helping a new baby into the world. I think that calls for actual plates and a glass of wine. You'll have to get another bottle for your next renters."

"It's fine." Milo walked to the table. His property manager always dropped off a bottle of red for the occupants. Milo would let him know that they needed another. It was the least of his concerns as Quinn's knee knocked against his.

Her shoulder-length hair was damp, and she was wearing borrowed clothes, but she was perfection. Her high cheekbones had a few freckles that his thumb ached to trace. How could he ask her if she'd ever thought of changing their relationship? If her heart had yearned like his for something more?

They ate in silence. The tension made Milo ache. Or maybe he was imagining it. After all, they hadn't eaten anything other than a few granola bars since their croissants this morning.

Once her plate was empty, Quinn leaned her

elbows on the table, propped her head in her palms, and stared at him. "We have a problem, you know."

Milo smiled. "We do?" Her full lips were calling to him. If she brought up the emotions charging the air around them, would it save him from having to find the right path to address their relationship? No. Thinking it through still held more appeal. Rushing only messed things up.

How many times did he have to prove that?

"Dishes!" She winked and pushed back from the table.

"Dishes?" Milo's head spun. "Dishes?" He hadn't meant to repeat the question, but his brain was incapable of finding any other response. He was thinking of kissing her, of changing everything, and Quinn was thinking about dishes?

Could he have misread the situation more?

Quinn leaned over and pecked his cheek. It was an innocent action. One she'd done hundreds of times over the years. "Yes." Her gaze held his as she gathered the plates and rose. "If we'd just eaten from the cartons, the cleanup would be so much easier."

"But the dinner would have been less satisfying," Milo murmured, standing, as well.

Like that peck?

It wasn't what he wanted. What he craved.

"Exactly!" Quinn's smile sent a thrill through him. "I've eaten off disposable plates in so many places. You don't realize what a luxury such simple things are until they aren't an option." She yawned, raising the plates over her head as she tried to cover the motion with her arm.

Milo took the dishes from her hands and laid them in the sink. "We've had a long day. I think they can wait until tomorrow."

She leaned against the counter, millimeters from him. "Today was certainly something."

Pushing the hair away from her left cheek, Milo nodded at her stitches. "And you got a permanent souvenir."

"A minor flaw. At least I'm presentable."

"No." Milo shook his head. "You are gorgeous." Without thinking, he let his fingers brush the softness of her cheek. Her skin was cool, but his fingers burned as he—finally—traced the line of freckles on her jaw. "Breathtaking. Smart. Courageous." *Sexy.* He barely caught that word. Over the years, he'd tried to combat the negativity he'd heard Quinn voice when she'd talked about herself. If only she could see what he saw. But tonight, so much more rested on his compliments.

Before his brain could comprehend what was happening, Quinn's lips connected with his.

Milo's arms wrapped around her waist and he pulled her to him. He didn't want any distance between them. Her fingers slid up his neck, ran through his hair, and Milo felt the world shift.

This was right. Quinn in his arms, her lips pressing against his. It made all reason leak from his brain.

Her mouth opened and a whole new level of sensations pulsed through him. She tasted of wine, Thai food and perfection.

His Quinn.

Wrapping a hand in her hair, Milo deepened the kiss. loving the small moans escaping her lips. He'd wondered how she kissed for months. Years…

Quinn…

Need pulled at him.

She pulled back a bit, her lips swollen. Her eyes were hooded with desire as she ran a finger down his jaw. "What are we doing?"

He couldn't read the expression floating through her eyes, and the first trace of doubt ripped down his back. What if she was just re-acting on the adrenaline from today?

"I don't know. Maybe making a mistake." Those were the wrong words. *Again.* He'd wanted this for so long, but her kiss had been so unexpected, so unplanned. He needed a plan— needed to know that she wanted more than just one night.

He knew Quinn didn't move from partner to partner. But he also knew she never stayed in one place too long, and he was tied to Califor-nia. The day had been crazy. What if…

"I—" Quinn stepped out of his arms. "Right." She shook her head. "Long day."

His arms felt heavy without her.

Why couldn't he say the right things?

"Quinn." Milo started toward her, but she put the counter between them.

"I'm going to..." Quinn looked to the back rooms. "Bed. Yep. I am going to bed. It was such a long day. I'm not acting like myself. Sorry."

Quinn rushed off before Milo could find a way to fix the mess his overthinking brain had caused. "Quinn." But she'd already fled down the hallway and closed the bedroom door.

"Dammit!" Milo gripped the counter, his brain too wired, too focused on Quinn, to let him sleep. Grabbing the wine bottle, he poured the last bit into his glass and stared at her closed door. Tomorrow... They'd sort all of this out tomorrow. At least he had a few hours to figure out a plan.

Quinn pushed a tear away from her cheek as she stared at the shadows cast by the rising sun along the beach. She'd left Milo's town house quietly, wishing there was some way she could make it home on her own. But her vehicle was back at St. Brigit's, almost two hours away.

How could she have been so stupid? It must have been the long day. And Milo telling her she was gorgeous. Leaning close...touching her cheek...

His compliments and touch had flooded her system. Flowed into the cracks her parents' harsh words and James's betrayal had worn on her soul. For just a moment, she'd believed Milo had been thinking the same thing she had been.

Quinn never let her guard down. She kept her shields up with everyone.

Everyone but Milo.

She could still feel the brush of his fingers along her cheek if she closed her eyes. *Gorgeous.* Had anyone ever called her that?

The emotion and desires that had raced through her since she'd landed in LA had propelled her forward with just a few compliments. Milo had always seen the best in her, looked past the flaws her mother and ex-fiancé had constantly pointed out. She was being needy, and she'd misread Milo's concern after a long day.

She wasn't bold with her partners. So Milo's rejection was the first she'd experienced—at least, before anything had actually happened. That was the only reason it burned so deeply.

She scoffed as the lie tripped through her brain. The truth was that it hurt because it was Milo. Because no matter what she tried to believe, Quinn wanted more.

And she hadn't even been able to seek refuge in her bungalow. Couldn't pretend to be busy for a few days while she licked her battered emotional wounds. Instead, she'd lain in bed knowing he was on the other side of the wall. So close and yet so far away.

Quinn hugged her knees as she buried her toes in the sand and stared at the ocean waves. She hadn't managed much sleep, but at least she'd worked out a plan to address last night's indiscretion. It would be easier if Milo didn't bring it up. She'd dated several men who would have let it go, but that was not Milo.

Milo planned everything. He'd want to talk about what had happened—make sure that she was all right. And he was going to apologize.

Shame tore across her. That was the part Quinn feared most. The "I'm sorry I don't feel the same. You're my best friend." She could hear the entire speech already, and the last thing she wanted was pity from Milo.

"You know, I tore through the place, afraid you'd started walking back to LA without telling me."

She started before offering a smile that Quinn prayed looked real in the early light. "How often do you get to watch the sunrise at the beach?" She gestured to the incoming waves as she accepted the travel mug of coffee he held out to her.

"You could have left a note." His voice was gruff as he slid down onto the sand beside her. He was grumpy this morning.

Not that she could blame him.

"A note? To walk four hundred feet from your front door to the beach?" She hit his shoulder with hers. If her plan was going to work, she needed to act as naturally as possible. "Really, Milo. I've come down here early before. Nothing has changed."

She said the final words and took a deep sip of her coffee, refusing to let her gaze leave the waves. He'd been her friend for decades and knew her better than anyone. If she looked at him, he might see the hurt pooling in her soul, and she couldn't let that happen.

"Nothing?" Milo's voice was soft. "We kissed last night."

"Actually, I kissed you." It hurt to say the words, but she kept her tone bright. For a minute last night, he'd responded to her. For that brief flicker, everything in her world had seemed right.

Quinn shook her head. She couldn't think of this now, not while sitting beside him. Not if her plan was to work. "I guess racing through a wildfire made me lose my head, huh? Flighty Quinn!"

"I hate it when you call yourself that." Milo's voice was ragged.

He'd loathed her family's nickname and despised the fact that she'd adopted the moniker.

But that didn't make it untrue. Quinn never stayed in one place too long. She made decisions based on a feeling in her gut, not rational thought. If a job felt right or didn't, she acted.

Even if everyone said it was a bad move.

She flew from relationships before she could get hurt, too.

That made it impossible to settle down and start a family.

Why wouldn't that chirp in her brain shut up? Quinn didn't have the close family she saw so many of her patients were blessed with. She'd never felt truly part of one, so she shouldn't miss it.

But she did.

And that was an ache that Milo's presence soothed.

But he'd pulled away from her last night. She wasn't sure that pain would ever vanish, but she couldn't lose Milo. He was the closest thing she had to family. She couldn't—wouldn't—risk that because her heart wanted something more. "At least now when people joke that they can't believe we've never kissed, we can say, 'Oh, we did once. We're just better as…friends.'"

She'd practiced that line before the sun rose this morning. Even with all that rehearsal, her voice still shook a bit.

"Better as friends," Milo murmured.

"Do you think I'm wrong?" She did look at

him then. Wished he'd contradict her. But Milo just stared at the incoming waves.

He hadn't shaved. The morning stubble along his jawline gave him a rugged look that made Quinn's stomach clench. Why did she have to be so attracted to him?

"You're all control and I'm all heart. You're planted here and I have rented furniture. We're opposites—perfectly balanced, but opposites." She kept waiting, hoping he'd interrupt her. He didn't. "I love St. Brigit's, but eventually…" She shrugged as she watched the waves crash against the beach.

"You do love finding new places." His head rested against hers as the sun cast its brilliant rays across the water.

You could ask me to stay…

She kept that desire buried deep inside. No one had ever asked Quinn to stay. Her family hadn't cared when she'd left for college and never come home. The men she'd dated had hardly batted their eyes when she'd taken a new position and packed up her things. Even James had barely blinked when she'd handed back his ring, no pleas for forgiveness or claims that he still wanted her. No one ever seemed to want her to stay.

"You have a world of adventures left," Milo said with a sigh as he straightened. Then he smiled and threw an arm around her shoulders. "And my life is in LA."

Quinn wanted to yank his arm away from her. Maybe that would stop the longing flowing through her. But he'd always touched her like that. In small ways that didn't mean much, even if she now wished they did. Leaning her head on his shoulder, Quinn sighed. She'd always planned to leave LA.

Hadn't she?

She'd rented her furniture but signed a two-year lease. The contradiction hadn't bothered her at the time. But leaving when her contract was up didn't feel like seeking adventure. Now it felt like running.

Maybe distance was what she needed, even if it was the last thing she wanted. If she stayed, she'd eventually make the same mistake she'd made last night. Let her feelings get too close to the surface and kiss him. She couldn't stand the thought of Milo pulling away again. That might just destroy her. For now, she would soak up as many of these moments as she could get. Maybe they'd be enough to last a lifetime.

Milo hadn't known the heart was capable of breaking before you actually dated someone. But as they walked the short distance back to his town house, that was the only description for the aching hole deep in his body. Quinn's actions had been impulsive. Brought on by yesterday's extremes.

He blew out a breath. How was he supposed to pretend that her touch hadn't electrified his soul? By remembering that this was just another stop for Quinn on her adventures and he was just lucky to be part of it. The reminder did little to quench the pull of need racing through him.

As they reached his door, Milo inhaled. The scent of the ocean gripped him. California was home. He'd never be the man who could pick up a phone and say yes to a job halfway around the world. He needed plans, schedules, five-year goals.

And he had those. All anchored in LA. He should focus on them. But right now, it was only Quinn that his brain wished to think of.

Quinn's ability to jump to a new adventure, to explore the next big thing, impressed him, even if he didn't understand it. But the realization that she would pack her bags again—maybe not today, or even this year, but someday—ripped him up.

He'd thrown his arm around her this morning because he'd wanted to touch her. To sit beside her for a few more minutes. As if his touch could anchor her. And because he was terrified she'd run from him after telling him that their kiss had been impulsive. When she'd leaned her head against his shoulder, it had taken every bit of his willpower not to kiss the top of it.

Her phone was ringing as he opened the door and she raced for it. Good, he needed a distraction.

"Hello?"

Milo walked over and poured himself another cup of coffee. He wasn't sure there was enough caffeine in the world to get him through the rest of the day. But he had to act unaffected by their morning chat. Otherwise, she might pick up and leave sooner—and Milo needed more time with her.

"Really?"

A smile tore across Quinn's face and Milo grinned despite himself. A happy Quinn thrilled him. No matter what happened between them, he wanted her to smile like that all the time. She clicked off the phone, and he raised an eyebrow.

"That was Martina. They're advising patients outside the LA city limits to seek care at our community partners, so they don't have to find a way around the evacuation zones—just to be safe. That means, until the all-clear comes through, all patients south of the city are advised to go to—"

Milo gripped the coffee cup, trying to ignore the twist in his gut. "Oceanside Clinic."

"Yep!"

"You seem surprisingly excited about this." He wanted to kick himself as Quinn's lips turned down.

Why was his brain refusing to find the right words?

"Sorry, Quinn. I didn't mean to make it sound like you were happy about any of this." Milo turned and started fixing another pot of coffee. At least his property manager stocked the cabinet with coffee and tea for the tenants. Otherwise, Milo would have been even more prickly this morning.

"You're right. It is a terrible time. But I've never gotten to work with your mom and Felix, assuming they want a few extra hands. Martina says we should exercise extreme caution in returning."

"I am certain my parents would love to have you help out."

And me, too.

His mother had tried repeatedly to get him to spend more time at the birthing center he'd helped design. She didn't understand his need to follow his father's dream, no matter how many times he'd discussed it.

It had led to a few tense arguments when she'd pointed out how happy the Oceanside Clinic made him. She was right. Milo enjoyed being there. But the closer he got to Felix, his mother's husband, the further his father slipped away. He was desperate to recapture the feelings he'd had so long ago.

Oceanside made him happy, but it would never bring him the same feeling he'd had with his father. He wasn't willing to give up that dream.

He couldn't.

"Are they as easy to work with as you?" Quinn's eyes were bright as she sidled up beside him and inhaled the scent of the brewing coffee.

"Easier," Milo remarked. It was the truth. His mother and Felix were the best physicians he'd ever worked with. The year he'd spent in their clinic following his divorce had been the happiest of his career—until Quinn had arrived at St. Brigit's.

Quinn's hip bumped his, and his body sang with the brief connection. "I'm not sure anyone is easier to work with than you. Any chance your mom might have scrubs I can borrow? She is almost as tall as me." Quinn folded her arms. "And we need transportation."

"Let me get another cup of coffee in me, Quinn. Then my mind will work a bit better. The sun's barely been up for more than an hour, in case you've forgotten."

"Nope," Quinn sighed. "I haven't forgotten." There was such a weariness to her statement.

Was she not as okay as she was pretending to be?

They'd always seemed to know what the other was thinking. But he couldn't stop second-guessing himself. Then she grinned, and Milo pushed the bead of hope from his mind. She was just Quinn. His perfect, fly-by-the-seat-of-her pants, explore-every-new-option, best friend, Quinn. And somehow that had to be enough.

CHAPTER FOUR

HIS PARENTS' CARS were already in the staff parking lot when Milo and Quinn's Uber driver dropped them at the back door. Quinn had traded the low-cut tank top from last night for one of the T-shirts he stashed at the town house for the few times he came down to surf.

His gray T-shirt was too big for Quinn. But she'd tied the corner of it, so it hugged her waist. It was a simple look, and it made his mouth water.

He needed to get control of himself. He'd lain in bed all night, aware that she was only a wall away, desperately trying to will his mind to do anything other than relive that kiss and his over-thinking, disastrous words.

Or fantasize about what could have come next.

"Quinn!" His mother raced for them and wrapped her arms around Quinn. They'd always been close, and he knew that Quinn had come to Oceanside several times since she'd moved to LA. They'd even come together—though not to the clinic.

When his mom stepped away from Quinn, she hugged him. "It is so good to see you—here, too." Her breath was warm on his chin as she kissed his cheek. "This is…" She paused, her lip wavering slightly. "Nice."

It wasn't what she'd meant to say. And Milo didn't have any problem hearing *This is where you belong*. It wasn't. But for the next few days or so, some of St. Brigit's patients were likely to show up at Oceanside.

"It's good to see you too, Mom." Milo threw an arm around her shoulder and squeezed it firmly before following her inside. "I fear we do not have anything other than us and our midwifery bags."

"Felix and I have scrubs for both of you. He drove his car today, so you can take mine back to LA."

"We can't—" Milo started.

"Are you planning to make Quinn walk back to LA, then?" His mother laughed as Quinn smiled.

"I… I hadn't figured that out yet." The phrase felt weird.

His mother's eyes widened. "You didn't spend all night working out the details?" She playfully put the back of her hand against his forehead. "You don't *feel* feverish."

Milo's gaze flitted to Quinn before he shook his head. "Nope. Yesterday was a bit of a beast.

You may not have heard, but we outran a wild-fire." His voice didn't sound as relaxed as he'd hoped. "I fell asleep as soon as I laid my head on the pillow."

Quinn's eyes flashed as the lie slipped from his tongue.

Rubbing his arms, Milo looked past his mother and Quinn. There was no way he was going to mention he'd spent the night replaying Quinn's kiss. That his brain had been incapable of focusing on anything substantive since their early-morning beach conversation.

"Well, lucky for you, I do have a plan." His mother wrapped an arm around Quinn. "Ladies' changing room is this way."

"You okay?"

Felix's deep voice made Milo jump. "You startled me!"

The lines deepened on Felix's brow. "Are you okay?" he repeated.

There wasn't much that got past Felix Ireman. He'd married Milo's mother not that long ago, and Milo and his sister, Gina, had been thrilled to welcome the man into their small family. But Milo wasn't going to talk to Felix about his roaring emotions for Quinn.

Substituting another concern, he shrugged. "I'm worried about my patients. Some of the staff will probably go to Bloom Birthing Center to help our patients that live north of the city, but it's a stressful time for everyone."

Felix nodded, though Milo suspected he didn't quite believe him. Luckily, Felix wasn't one to pry. "Well, we're glad you're here. Did your mother mention that Dr. Acton's husband was transferred last month, and they're away on a house-hunting expedition in Ohio? She'll be hard to replace."

The statement hit Milo in the chest. "I'm sure you'll find the right person," he said, turning to find his own set of scrubs before Felix could raise the subject of Milo returning to Oceanside.

Quinn and Milo had been assigned to the birthing center and Sherrie had joined them from St. Brigit's. At least Milo's parents' clinic was well equipped to handle the influx of patients.

Soothing music played in the hallways. The walls were painted a light gray, but Gina, Milo's sister, had ensured the effect was calming, not sterile. Having an interior designer in the family had clearly come in handy when Milo had developed the plans for the birthing center.

Quinn could still remember his excitement as he'd laid out the basic plan when they were undergrads. He'd even asked Quinn to sketch a few of the ideas for him, even though her drawing skills favored landscapes.

The architects had adjusted the design, but the

basics of what Milo had imagined were all here. She'd been in Hawaii when they'd broken ground on the facility, and on the island of Tonga when they'd held the ribbon-cutting ceremony, so she'd only seen it in pictures.

It was perfect. A calmness settled through her that was so at odds with the craziness of the last day. This place was lovely. A truly great accomplishment. And yet, Milo hadn't stayed long enough to see the ribbon-cutting two years ago. Quinn shook her head.

"Something wrong?" Milo's voice was soft as he stepped beside her. What was it about places where babies were born that made everyone, even the midwives and doctors who routinely saw births, lower their voices?

Yes, her heart screamed. So many things were wrong. He didn't want her. He wasn't working in the center that he'd helped design. And she felt like this was home.

All those things bothered her, but that final piece struck her harder than she'd expected. She'd worked many places. And enjoyed something about all of them. But she'd never walked into a birthing center, hospital or field hospital, and felt a sense of peace. A sense of rightness.

Like this was where she was meant to be.

It was ridiculous, of course. This was Milo's place, even if he didn't work here.

Yet…

He'd do well at a large facility, maybe even run Valley General's OB unit for a few years, but this was the place he'd come home to eventually. She knew it deep in her soul.

She belonged here, too. But she didn't know what that meant for their friendship after last night. *If anything.* But she couldn't push the feeling from her heart.

"Just marveling at your work." Quinn sighed as she looked at him. Her arms ached to reach out to him. To smooth the creases from his forehead. At least at work she could focus on keeping a professional distance.

"It's more my mother's work and my sister's interior decorating. I think it could use a splash of color. Maybe not bright yellow, but…" Milo's words ran out.

He rubbed the back of his neck before smiling. He was trying to be normal, too. Maybe in a day or two, it wouldn't feel so awkward between them—though she knew that was just wishful thinking. Nothing would ever be the same.

At least not for her.

"No picking on my kitchen." Her throat seized. What if her kitchen was gone? "That color makes me happy."

Straightening her shoulders, she forced the subject back to the Oceanside Clinic. "But this is your accomplishment, Milo. It wouldn't be here without you."

Milo's lips turned up as he looked around. "It is nice."

Nice? Was that the word he associated with it? This place was wonderful. A birthing center that gave mothers more choices in their delivery options, run by OBs, with a surgical suite tucked out of sight in case of emergency deliveries. Already a few hospital administrators from California, Ohio and Texas had visited to see if they could mimic Oceanside's successes. *Nice* didn't begin to cover this achievement.

The buzzer at the front of the building rang out and she was grateful for the interruption. "Incoming." Quinn smiled. She loved deliveries. New life was the best part of her job. And it was the perfect distraction.

A woman wearing a floral-print dress walked in holding the arm of a tall man who was clearly more distressed than his partner. "Hello." The woman smiled and gasped in a breath as she started to work through a contraction.

"We're having a baby!" her partner nearly shouted.

Quinn smiled. "Are you sure?" She walked over to the woman and playfully looked at her belly.

"I think so." The woman let out a giggle and tapped her partner's side. "You have to let go of me for a few minutes, sweetheart." She rose on her tiptoes and kissed his cheek.

He laid his hands over her belly, and Quinn's heart leaped at the simple motion.

This was what her life was missing. Family.

Her friendship with Milo was nice—better than nice when things weren't so tense between them—but it wasn't the sense of belonging she experienced with her patients. Wasn't what her soul yearned for.

Pushing the feeling away, she gestured for the mother to follow her while her partner checked them in. The young woman looked back at him, and Quinn squeezed her hand. "Dr. Russell will settle him down. I promise."

Milo was already talking to the father while the admitting nurse kept passing him electronic forms to sign. By the time the father was ready to join them in a few minutes, Milo would have soothed all his worries.

If only Quinn could soothe away her feelings that way, too.

"You're not Dr. Russell or Dr. Acton." The man looked around him. Milo could see the happiness and hope bubbling through him. All new parents seemed to wear that expression. But there was a layer of fear beneath the surface, too. Many first-time parents were fearful, but anxiety poured from this man as he bounced on his heel and kept his gaze on the hallway where his partner had disappeared.

"Actually, I am a Dr. Russell. Dr. Milo Russell. I'm an OB, like my mother. I'm filling in for Dr. Acton while she is out today. And you are?"

"Trey Kenns."

The man bit his lip as he stared at Milo. Keeping his voice low, Milo leaned closer. "Trey, your wife will be fine."

"Fiancée." The man's fingers trembled as he electronically signed another document. "We… we…" He sighed loudly. "None of this was planned. But it's amazing."

Milo blinked. He'd attended more than one birth where the partner didn't seem as thrilled about the birth as he'd thought they should be. But this man was clearly excited…and terrified. "What wasn't supposed to happen?"

"Carla and I were best friends. *Are* best friends." He looked toward the hallway where his fiancée had disappeared. "Took me months to convince her that we should be…" He pushed his hair back. "Sorry, I ramble when I'm nervous. I never planned to have children. If I lose her…"

Recognition flew through Milo. "You lost someone in childbirth?"

Trey nodded. "My mother and baby sister. It's been years, and I know the technology is better. But you ever had someone that meant the world to you?"

Yes. And she was with Trey's fiancée right now. Milo nodded. "She'll be fine. I promise. Quinn

Davis is one of the finest midwives in the world. And that is not me exaggerating. She's served all over the globe. Carla is in excellent hands. And if, for some reason, we need it, we have a surgical suite for emergency C-sections, if necessary. But less than six percent of birthing center deliveries result in C-sections. She and your baby are in excellent hands."

Slapping Trey on the back, he motioned for the soon-to-be dad to follow him. "I think Kelly has had you fill out all the paperwork for admittance. Why don't we go see how Carla is progressing?"

Quinn stepped out of Carla's room and wiped a bead of sweat from her forehead. Milo started toward her without thinking. Carla had been in labor for most of the day, but Quinn hadn't raised any concerns to him. The two times he'd checked on her, Carla had been progressing slowly, but progressing.

"Everything okay?" Milo saw the tightness in Quinn's shoulders. They'd been running on full steam since Molly's delivery. How was that only two days ago?

"She's finally at seven centimeters. With any luck, Carla will move into transition labor soon. But she's been laboring for almost twelve hours already. Not counting the six hours she did at home. She's getting tired."

Milo knew that was an understatement. Carla

had to be exhausted. A woman's ability to deliver after a long labor never failed to impress him, but if she got too tired…

"Are you worried?"

He hadn't lied to Trey. Quinn was an excellent midwife. She'd been on multiple tours with Doctors Without Borders, spent more than a decade as a traveling nurse, and always seemed to find her way to where she was needed most. She'd delivered babies all over the world and in conditions far less comfortable than this. Her instincts were almost always spot-on.

"No." Quinn shook her head. "At least, not yet. If she doesn't move into transitional labor in the next hour or two, I may adjust that statement."

Milo nodded as he leaned against the wall beside her. His skin vibrated at the closeness, and his palms ached with the desire to reach for her. Holding her hand, putting an arm around her shoulder or her waist—anything. Even after what had happened this morning, he couldn't stand the idea of being away from Quinn. Thank goodness, they were at work or his heart might just give in.

Putting distance between them would probably be a good idea. And a hell of a lot easier if they weren't working and staying in the same apartment. But Milo didn't want to change things. Maybe when she took off for parts unknown again, he'd find a way to adjust. Right now, though, he couldn't bear the thought of it.

"How is Trey?" He'd only seen Carla's fiancé a few times as he'd run for ice chips—literally run! One of the floor nurses had warned him to use his walking feet, and Milo had laughed.

"They are adorable," Quinn breathed. "They have been best friends since high school. I swear they even seem to be able to read each other's thoughts. Just like…" She turned her face from his and let the words die away.

Just like us…

The unspoken words hung in the space between them. Milo swallowed the lump in his throat as he tried to force air into his lungs. He should say something, but his brain disconnected from his tongue as the silence dragged on.

She cleared her throat. "Anyway…they started dating about nine months ago." Quinn grinned as she tried to rub the knots out of her neck.

"Ah." Milo chuckled. "Well, they seem very happy." He hated the twinge of jealousy pooling in his gut. He just needed to focus on his goals, his plans, focus on the feeling they gave him. Except, for the first time, planning out his life didn't offer him any comfort.

"Breathe," Quinn ordered Carla as Trey held her hand.

Milo had entered when Carla had started pushing. The baby's heart rate had dropped the first time she'd pushed. Early decelerations often hap-

pened when the baby's head was compressed in
the birth canal.

The heart rate had stabilized, and it hadn't
happened again. But Milo was on standby, monitoring for any sign of fetal distress. He had also
ordered the surgical suite readied—just in case.

He was probably overthinking this delivery,
but the hairs on the back of his neck were rising.
He'd promised Trey that Carla would be fine. A
promise he made to all his patients, but the reality was that labor could be dangerous. There was
a reason it was still the highest cause of death for
women in underdeveloped countries. Technology lessened that burden, but it didn't decrease
it altogether.

Milo had lost a few patients during his career. It was impossible to work in this field for
years and not have at least a handful of deliveries go wrong. But today was not going to be one
of those days.

"The next contraction is coming, I need you
to push, Carla." Quinn's voice was tight as she
looked at the maternal and fetal heart rate monitors. "Dr. Russell."

That sent a chill down his spine. During deliveries, Quinn maintained an informality with
him. Except when there was a problem. Then he
immediately became "Dr. Russell." It was her
tell. He wasn't even sure she was aware of it.

His eyes flicked to the heart monitor. The baby's heart rate had shifted from early deceleration to variable deceleration. The baby wasn't getting enough oxygen.

"Carla, I want you to lay back until the next contraction comes." Milo nodded to Trey. "Help her lie back."

"What's going on?" Trey's voice was shaky as he looked from Quinn to Milo.

"The baby's heart rate is fluctuating in a way that I don't like," Milo said. "The little guy has been holding steady throughout labor, so adjusting your position a bit might be enough to give him the room he needs."

"And if it doesn't?" Carla's voice was firm as she gripped Trey's hand and looked at Quinn.

"Then Dr. Russell will perform an emergency C-section." Quinn's voice was low as she stared at the monitors.

She looked at him, and Milo saw the steel in Quinn again. But a subtle peace pressed against him. They were partners, maybe not romantically, but for the first time since she'd walked away from him last night, Milo felt like he could truly breathe.

She held up one finger. This was where their closeness, their friendship, and the layers beneath it collided. The benefits of being able to read each other so easily. Quinn was willing to let Carla push one more time, but if the baby's heart rate dropped again, they'd transfer her to the surgical suite. He nodded and she turned back to their patient.

"All right, Carla. Push on the next contraction, but if your baby's heart rate drops, Dr. Russell will get ready for a C-section."

"My baby?"

"Can be here in less than fifteen minutes, if necessary," Milo stated as he watched the monitors.

"Don't tell him I said so, but Dr. Russell is one of the best in the business." Quinn smiled as she fake whispered the compliment.

He felt his lips tip up. Quinn didn't issue false praise. Her confidence in him sent a wave of strength through Milo. She'd never doubted his ability to accomplish anything. She'd always been his biggest cheerleader. Maybe they were opposites, but they complemented each other— she was right about that.

"Try to breathe regularly," Milo instructed. The baby's heart rate shifted, and Milo exchanged a look with Quinn. The rate hadn't dropped nearly as much on that contraction as it had on the previous one, but it had fallen. They needed to get Carla and Trey's son out now.

Quinn nodded at Milo, and he took a deep breath. "Carla, we are transferring you."

"This wasn't part of the plan." Trey's voice wobbled as he watched Quinn prep Carla's bed for transfer.

"Trey, a nurse will be back to get you in a few minutes." Quinn pulled Carla's bed forward.

Milo didn't have time to comfort the man, but he offered a small smile to Carla's fiancé.

Trey dropped a light kiss on her forehead. "I'll see you soon."

"I'll be the one on the operating table." The love radiating between them was so apparent.

"Here we go," Quinn called as she guided the bed out of the room.

Fifteen minutes later, Milo listened to the monitors as he lifted Carla's son from her exposed womb. The umbilical cord was wrapped around the boy's neck and his skin had a blue hue. Milo unwrapped the cord, but still, the little guy made no noise.

"He's not crying." Trey's voice echoed in the room.

"Trey..." Carla's voice wobbled through the curtain separating them. "Why is he not crying, Quinn?"

"Give the little guy a minute. He's been through a time." Quinn's voice was low but comforting as she took the newborn from Milo, wrapped him in a warm towel, and started rubbing his back.

Come on, little one.

Milo kept his eyes on Carla's incisions and his ears tuned to the baby and Quinn.

After what seemed like an eternity, but was probably no more than a few seconds, the tiny man let out one of the angriest wails Milo could ever remember hearing. Quinn's gaze met his as she laid the baby on Carla's chest.

"He's got a full head of hair." Quinn grinned as she looked from Carla to Trey to Milo.

There was no one he'd rather be in a delivery room or surgical suite with than Quinn. No one he'd rather be with anywhere. Milo let out a breath and smiled as he finished closing Carla's incisions.

Looking over the curtain, he stared at the small family. Trey looked at them with such love that Milo felt his chest clamp. He loved helping deliver new life, and he'd never felt envious of anyone before, but as he looked from Carla and Trey to Quinn, he was surprised by the twinge of the emotion pulling at him.

Maybe her kissing him had been impulsive, but Milo suddenly didn't care. In that moment, she'd wanted him. There were tons of adventures they could have together in California. Milo just needed to find a way to make her want to stay.

With him.

CHAPTER FIVE

"IF THIS GOES on much longer, we will need to get a few more clothes," Quinn joked as she dumped the small load of laundry on Milo's leather couch. Her shoulders were knotted, and she flexed them twice before picking up the gray T-shirt Milo had loaned her. Between monitoring her phone for any word that she could return home, and trying her best to act normal around her best friend, Quinn's entire body felt like it might snap.

Milo picked up another shirt and started folding it. "That is true, but this has been nice, too."

Quinn raised an eyebrow. Nice? That was not a description she'd use to describe the last three days. Though last night, when they'd watched a movie, it had almost felt like old times.

Except it hadn't at all… Her heart had screamed as her brain tried to rationalize the hour and a half she'd spent wondering if she was acting normal enough. Or too normal. Or any of the other myriad thoughts that had run through her head.

This was what needy felt like, and Quinn hated it. Her mother had called her "needy" if she broke any rule or asked to do anything other than approved extracurricular activities. Her wants were too much. And each time she'd failed to follow her parents' exacting rules, she'd been belittled. Her schedule and her life had never truly been her own.

Even the drawing classes she'd begged for had only been granted after her art teacher had told them she was skilled. However, instead of taking classes at the local community center, her mother had set her up with a private art teacher four times a week. The thing Quinn had loved most became a controlled item on her schedule, not an activity she could actually lose herself in.

Yet as each day of uncertainty with Milo dragged on, Quinn wished she had some way to manage the chaos.

But would it ease the uncertainty or make her feel trapped?

Softly exhaling, Quinn forced those thoughts to the side. "'Nice'? How do you figure?"

Milo dragged a hand across the back of his neck. "Quinn…"

His deep voice sent a tingle down her back. He leaned toward her, and she held her breath. The drop of hope that he might kiss her had refused to die. It was ridiculous, and if she was able to spend more time away from him, then she might be able to bury it completely. But as his green eyes held hers, she couldn't quiet the want pulsating in her chest.

"I like spending time with you." Milo's words were soft.

Quinn let out a nervous laugh. She liked spending time with him, too, always had. He'd never made her feel unwanted...until two nights ago. Her stomach flipped as she focused on the laundry again. "Milo, we are always together. *Literally.* We work together, and you were at my bungalow almost every weekend."

"Yes." Milo's hip connected with hers. The touch was too much and not enough all at once. "I had to come to the bungalow," Milo continued, oblivious to the turmoil roiling through her, "you never came to my place."

"That is not true." Quinn's head popped back. She'd gone to his place when she'd first returned. And been anxious from the moment she'd stepped into it until she'd left.

The downtown high-rise unit looked like something out of a design magazine. Its light gray walls were devoid of pictures. Flower vases, filled with fake arrangements, hovered in the corners, adding the appropriate hints of color against the perfectly oiled hardwood floors. It screamed success. But it wasn't personal.

Her mother would have loved the place. She'd have oohed and aahed at the full-length windows that overlooked downtown. Complimented the well-thought-out vases and minimalistic decor that made the space look bigger than it was. *Upscale*... That was the description she would have used.

Quinn had felt out of place in her torn blue jeans and T-shirt. A lackluster accessory to Milo's life on the fast track to success. After all, what did she have to show for the last ten years? All her worldly possessions had fit into the two canvas bags she'd carried when she'd landed in LA.

Sure, her bank account was healthy, but it couldn't afford the rent for a downtown unit like Milo's. Not that she'd told him that. The few places that he'd scoped out for her had been nice, but they'd also been too much for her—too upscale.

"Really?" Milo's lip quirked. "I don't think one time counts, Quinn."

Why was he pushing this?

He'd always seemed fine coming to her place. "I was there at least twice." When Milo playfully rolled his eyes, Quinn shrugged. "It's too clean!"

"You're complaining about my cleanliness?" Milo laughed. "Should I have had dirty laundry draped over the couch or dirty dishes in the sink? Somehow I don't think that would be very enticing."

His voice shifted; its deepness almost felt like

it was stroking her. The gleam in his eye and the dimple in his cheek sent thrills through her.

Was he flirting with her?

It was a ridiculous thought, but as his gaze held hers, she almost thought he was.

"No!" Quinn lightly slapped his shoulder. And her fingers burned from the brief connection. She needed to stop touching him. But that was an edict her body refused to follow.

"I should've picked a different adjective. It's perfect. Airy." She put a finger to her chin. "Picturesque. That is the word for it. I worry that if I spill anything, I might destroy the esthetic. Then I won't be invited again."

Milo's strong arms encompassed her. And before she could catch herself, Quinn leaned her head against his shoulder. "You are always welcome at my place, Quinn. Always and forever."

Forever. A term Quinn never associated with anyone.

No, that wasn't true.

She'd always associated it with Milo.

Milo's fingers moved along her back, and Quinn sighed. This hug was dangerous. His heat poured through her as she cataloged each finger's small stroke. She inhaled, letting his scent rip through her.

Milo...

She looked up and met his eyes, but he didn't release her. His gaze hovered on her lips.

Or maybe she just wished it would.

She tried to force her feet to move, but they were unwilling to follow her brain's command.

She sighed as Milo smiled at her. Just a moment longer...

"Quinn—"

Before Milo could finish whatever he'd planned to say, Quinn's phone rang. Grateful for the distraction, she pulled away.

The area code sent waves of excitement and dread racing down her spine. This was the call she'd been waiting for. But her fingers cramped as she stared at the answer button. The oxygen had evaporated from the room. The issues with Milo...the fire...all of it was just too much.

She slapped the phone into his hand. "I can't answer. Please."

Milo pursed his lips then lifted the phone to his ear.

Before he could do more than just say hello, Quinn bolted. It was childish, but she needed a moment to prepare for whatever Milo learned. Prepare for where she'd go if the tiny number of personal items she'd treasured were gone.

Her toes hit the sand of the beach and Quinn leaned over her knees. "Get yourself together. Get yourself together. You can handle this. You have to."

Quinn repeated the mantra to herself over and over, trying to put her feelings back behind the walls she'd carefully constructed since her child-hood. Why were they cracking now—when she needed them the most?

Milo clicked off the call and looked toward the door. Her shoes were still there, so she couldn't have gone anywhere other than the beach. He couldn't blame her for not wanting to hear the message. Though the recording hadn't said much, the fire was now under control in her area and residents could return starting this afternoon.

Miranda had also called to let them know that St. Brigit's was no longer referring patients to other clinics. They could head home to Los Angeles.

He just didn't know exactly what home looked like now.

But they'd figure that out together.

He headed for the beach.

Quinn was standing at the edge of the ocean, her back to him. He stared at her for a few minutes. Her shoulders were tight, and he knew that he'd added to that strain. But everything had shifted and he didn't want it to go back to normal. Not with Quinn.

They belonged together. She knew everything about him, they completed each other's sentences and the first call they made when their worlds exploded was always to one another. Maybe his brain had overthought her impulsive kiss, but Quinn moved with her heart.

And it had reached out to him.

There were still a few months left on Quinn's contract with St. Brigit's. There was plenty of time for him to make her realize she belonged here—*with him*. But first, they needed to go to her place and see if there was anything left.

"One step at a time," Milo muttered as he stepped onto the beach.

"How bad is it?" Quinn's voice was ragged.

She turned to him as she brushed a tear from her cheek. The single tear tore his heart. Had he ever seen Quinn cry?

No.

Quinn refused to show that weakness. Even when her parents had been awful, and then when they'd passed and the opportunity to ever achieve some reconciliation had evaporated, no tears had spilled from Quinn's eyes. He'd known that the bungalow meant a lot to her, but Milo hadn't realized how much the place had touched her.

She wrapped her arms around his waist. "Just tell me."

"I don't know." He laid his head against her head, wishing he could put an end to the unknown. Hating that this horrible situation she was facing gave him an excuse to touch her.

He dropped a kiss to the top of her head without thinking and was grateful when she didn't pull away. If they could stand on the beach holding each other forever, he'd be the happiest man ever. But life called, and they needed to see to the next steps. "That was just the notification that the fire is contained enough for us to return this afternoon."

Quinn ran her hands through her hair and cringed. "This is the worst Schrödinger's cat situation. Is my house still around? Or do I have nothing? Nowhere to go?"

"You will *never* have nowhere to go, Quinn." Milo squeezed her tightly, wishing there was a way to take all the pain and worry from her.

How could she think about going anywhere but to his place?

"I hope your bungalow is unharmed. But Quinn—" he squeezed her tightly "—you will always have a place with me."

"I know." Quinn smiled, but it didn't quite reach her eyes. The wind caught her hair as she stared at him. "I'm just worried and trying to bury my neediness."

Her eyes widened, and Milo doubted she'd meant to say that. "Being worried about your home isn't neediness, Quinn. And everyone is needy sometimes."

"Thank you," she sighed.

"Miranda called, too. Looks like we've worked our last shifts at my parents' clinic. The fire is contained enough for everyone to make it safely to St. Brigit's." The words were sooty in his mouth. He'd enjoyed working at Oceanside again. Loved being near his family.

"Well, right now, I am trying to figure out how to get back to the town house without dragging sand everywhere. Standing in the ocean seemed like such a good idea a few minutes ago."

Milo had worn sandals down to the beach. This was something he could fix. "Hop on!" He turned and pointed to his back.

"No!" Quinn laughed. "I'm too tall and heavy."

"Are you calling me weak?" Milo grinned as he looked over his shoulder at her. These were the moments he lived for; being with her, making her laugh even as life's chaos twisted around them. He wanted years of laughter and fun with her.

"Very funny." Quinn glared at him.

Another wave rolled over her feet, and he hopped just far enough away to keep his feet from getting wet. He was going to have a bit of sand on his sandals, a small price to pay for living so close to the beach.

Except you don't live here anymore, his brain reminded him.

"Either you're going to have to walk through the sand with wet feet, or you'll have to get on my back. Come on, Quinn."

"Fine. But if I break you, you can't complain

about it." Quinn wagged her finger before accepting his offer.

"You could never break me," Milo stated with more bravado than he felt. Quinn was light enough on his back. But she had the power to destroy him.

They were best friends, but so much more. She was the person who knew him better than anyone else. The woman who had made him smile when his marriage had failed. The person who'd answer his phone calls no matter which time zone she was in. She could tell his moods and always find a way to make him feel better. Quinn was the other part of his heart.

But what if she didn't feel the same way?

Milo pushed that worry away.

Hope slipped away as Quinn stared at the ashes around them as she and Milo made their way toward where her bungalow should be. The hills that had once been dotted with older homes and small lawns were now unrecognizable. Quinn was grateful that Milo had insisted on driving. Not only because her hands were shaking, but because she wasn't sure she could have found her way here.

All the landmarks she'd associated with the area were gone. She could have relied on GPS, sure, but she probably wouldn't have thought to turn it on until she'd been turned around a few times. Quinn had worked in multiple disaster zones, seen people deal with the trauma of losing everything, but she hadn't been prepared for this. No one could be.

Milo's hand reached for hers and Quinn held it tightly. "I am so sorry, Quinn."

As he slowed the car, Quinn realized they'd turned down her street. Everything was gone. A small sob escaped her lips. Her parents hadn't allowed her to have many possessions as a child. At least, not things that mattered to a small child, like drawings from school or pictures she liked. She'd never developed a desire for worldly goods. But seeing what little she did have turned to gray dust stung.

She had renter's insurance and—thankfully—had added wildfire protection, but the pictures of her and Milo all dressed up for their undergraduate graduation, pictures and notes from friends around the world, the few mementos she'd saved from her childhood. No amount of insurance could replace those.

She leaned her head against the headrest. Her body was heavy. Quinn had thought she was ready for this. She'd known what might happen when the mandatory evacuation had been issued. But seeing the destruction sent waves of panic through her.

What was she going to do?

"Do you want to go?" Milo's voice was gen-

tle as his fingers stroked hers. "We don't have
to look through the ashes. At least, not today. If
anything is left..." His voice died away, but he
didn't release her hand.

She wanted to run—wanted to get away from
the week's stresses and hurts. But the sooner she
got through this part, the sooner she could start
to grieve for what was gone.

At least Milo is here.

"No, let's get this over with. I don't think I can
do this alone." The confession slipped through
her lips. She'd traveled the world, landed in new
places and handled all of life's challenges alone.
It was something Quinn took pride in.

But her ability to control herself, to lock away
her emotions, had evaporated. Her face heated,
but she kept her eyes firmly closed. It was the
truth, and her walls were piles of ash at this point
anyway.

"You never have to do anything alone, Quinn."
Milo's arms suddenly enveloped her. "Never."

The car was small, and the action felt awkward, but comfort swam through her. She only
allowed herself a cycle of breath before she
pulled back. "Thank you."

Gripping the door handle, she looked at the
destroyed lot that had once been her bungalow.
"Let's go see if the fire left anything. Then, do
you mind dropping me at a clothing store? I'd
like something other than Bianca's leftovers."

"Of course." Milo nodded. "But I am not dropping you anywhere. If you need to go to twenty different stores, I will go to each one with you."

She should say something, thank him for the kind statement, but her tongue was heavy and her brain lacked words. Opening the car door, she let out a soft cry. The world smelled of smoke and destroyed dreams.

But Quinn forced her feet to move forward. She could do this. Had to.

Walking up the singed cement walkway, Quinn stared at the fallen stucco walls and wet soot. She stepped over a pile of debris as she stood in what was once her living room, though there was nothing to identify it.

Swallowing, she turned to find Milo. His face was long, but he was pushing at the ashes with his feet. She needed to do the same, to see if there was anything that she might be able to salvage. But where to start?

The garage... The boxes she'd set there and then forgotten in her rush to get to Molly's delivery had been full of papers and trinkets that wouldn't have stood a chance in the blaze. But she had to check.

Please...

The metal door frame that had led to the tiny garage was still standing. A spooky host to a door that had burned. A doorway to nowhere.

Quinn shivered despite the afternoon's heat. Watching her step, she moved toward the marker.

Squatting, she brushed away the ashes that had once been her most precious things. Biting her lip, Quinn sucked in air. They were just things… The phrase felt hollow. They were her memories, and now they lived entirely in her mind.

Her fingers caught on something sharp and Quinn let out a small cry. Pulling her hand back, she looked it over. No blood or scratches.

"Quinn?"

Milo's voice carried across the damage, but she ignored him. Something besides soot and ash was there. It was probably part of the ceiling or a chunk of wall, but…

An ironwork frame emerged from the destruction and she let out another low cry. This time her heart was rejoicing. The frame was singed, and the glass darkened, but there in the frame was the image of her and Milo holding up her nursing diploma.

Her family hadn't attended her graduation. Her father had claimed a big work meeting that he couldn't miss and her mother had made an excuse so ridiculous that Quinn had long ago dumped it from her memory. But Milo had waited for hours before the civic hall opened to make sure he could sit in the front row.

Her lip trembled as she stared at the photograph. It was dirty, the corners burned. It would never look pristine again, but it was safe.

"I still remember how big your smile was when you walked across the stage." Milo's voice was low as he knelt next to her. "You were radiant. I remember the exact moment your gaze caught mine." Milo smiled as he looked at the photo.

Radiant... Her throat tightened as she clasped the picture to her chest. *What was he doing?*

She kept that question buried in her heart as she stared at the rest of the debris pile. "I think this is the only thing that survived."

"I found a few pots, though they are a bit less cylindrical now. And one spoon." Milo wrapped an arm around her shoulders. "But I didn't make it back to your bedroom. Did you have any pictures there?"

"No." Quinn blinked back the moisture coating her eyes. She was not going to cry, "I put all the photos I treasured by the door. When Molly went into labor, I left. Guess I figured I'd get another chance."

Milo's nose scrunched. She pressed her hand against his cheek, not caring about the soot stain she was leaving. Quinn needed to touch him, needed to ground them. "What's wrong?"

He raised an eyebrow. "Speaking of another chance—" Before he could finish, a scream went up from the house, or what was left of it, a few doors down.

"Help!" The call was cracked and laced with terror.

Milo took off. Quinn laid the picture down and raced after him.

Mrs. Garcia was hovering over her husband near the front steps of what had once been their well-maintained porch. Her hands were covered in blood.

Milo reached them, and Quinn pulled out her phone to call 9-1-1 as she turned and raced back to the car. There was water there, and they'd brought their midwifery bags with them. They had sterile gauze and a few supplies that might be useful until the ambulance arrived.

By the time she returned, she had a stitch in her side, but Mr. Garcia was sitting up. The right side of his face was streaked with blood, and the cut running up his leg would need to be cleaned at the hospital and closed with at least a dozen stitches. It was still seeping blood.

"Is it slowing at all?" Quinn asked as she slipped in next to Milo.

"No." He took the water and hand sanitizer she offered. It wasn't much, but it was better than nothing. Milo laid several gauze pads across the wound before pulling off his T-shirt and pressing it against the wound, as well.

She glanced at Milo as she sanitized her own

hands and donned gloves. His muscles were taut as he kept pressure on Mr. Garcia's wound. He hadn't hesitated to act. His quick thinking would have been a benefit in many of the field hospitals she'd served in.

And they were a giant benefit here, too.

"The ambulance is at least fifteen minutes out." Quinn kept her voice low, but she heard Mrs. Garcia whimper. In an area with well-known traffic issues, fifteen minutes wasn't terrible. Still, everyone knew that it might take longer.

Milo nodded. "I think the bleeding is slowing, but there is at least one vein open, up by the knee."

Pulling out the surgical tape that they carried in their bags, Quinn wrapped it tightly around the shirt. She and Milo needed both their hands. This way, pressure would remain on the wound.

"What happened?" Milo asked as he moved his attention from Mr. Garcia's leg to his head.

"He insisted we come back for some silly trinket that he forgot to pack." Mrs. Garcia bit her lip as she stared at her husband.

Quinn offered her a forgiving look. "I think Milo was asking about what happened with the injury."

"I…" Mr. Garcia huffed as he gestured to the house and started over. "The steps were loose and crumbled when I stepped on them. Guess the fire was hot enough to weaken the cement." He blinked and moved to touch his face before Milo caught his arm.

"Let me." His voice was low and soothing, but still authoritative. Even in this destroyed area, shirtless, with nothing but a midwifery bag and bottles of water, Milo was the consummate professional.

Quinn bit her lip as Milo carefully cleaned the cut on Mr. Garcia's head. His gentle touches made Quinn's heart clench. She'd loved working with him. It wasn't St. Brigit's, or the wonderful work being done there, that had called her home. It was Milo and how complete she felt when she was near him.

Milo was the reason her walls were in such shambles. She'd never kept them up around him. She'd always been herself. Maybe it would be safer for her heart to find a way to erect them, but Quinn didn't want to. Not now or ever.

"And it wasn't a trinket." Mr. Garcia's voice was strong as he looked at his wife. "It was your anniversary present. I spent months making…"

He looked over Quinn's shoulder. "I didn't expect this level of destruction. Even with the news reports, somehow…" He closed his eyes.

Mrs. Garcia's eyes widened. "We are here for an anniversary present? I could throttle you." Then her gaze softened. "Right after I kiss you."

"I almost lost you once, honey. I won't risk

it again." Mr. Garcia's eyes were full of love as they looked at his wife.

"Almost lost her?" The question slipped from Quinn's lips as she checked on Mr. Garcia's leg. It was still bleeding, but blood wasn't seeping through Milo's T-shirt. Though Quinn had waved to Mrs. Garcia whenever she saw the woman puttering around in her yard, they were not close. Certainly not close enough for her to pry into their private lives.

Mrs. Garcia laughed as she folded her arms. "It's his running joke. I asked him out first. I was very brazen in my youth, although I'm more so now, if I may say so." She winked at her husband. The silly gesture felt oddly intimate. The kind of inside joke that long-married, happy couples enjoyed.

"Gumption," Mr. Garcia corrected. "She had—*has* so much gumption."

"Anyway…" Her eyes never left her husband's face as she retold what was obviously a well-discussed memory between them. "I asked him out, and he said no."

Milo's breath hitched and Quinn's chest tightened. She made sure to keep her face averted.

What was he thinking?

"I was so surprised that the prettiest girl I'd ever seen wanted me. I thought it was a joke. Biggest mistake of my life." Mr. Garcia sighed as he stared at his wife.

The sirens rang out in the distance, and Quinn saw Mrs. Garcia's shoulders relax. She understood. She'd be glad when they were on their way to get his leg properly looked at, too.

"It took me almost a month to work up the courage to own up to the mistake." Mr. Garcia wrapped his hand around his wife's wrist.

Quinn felt moisture form along the ridges of her eyelashes—again. She was in danger of becoming a real watering pot.

She saw Milo catch her gaze and watched an unknown emotion play across his face. She wanted to believe that it was desire, hope for a different future than they'd discussed on the beach. A second chance…

She'd played his little touches and jokes from this morning over in her head. She was almost positive he'd been flirting. Milo never did anything without thinking it out.

There'd been so much going on the day she'd kissed him. What if she broached the topic again when life wasn't so hectic? When he could think about it for a few minutes? If he turned her down then, at least she'd never wonder what-if—even if it left a crater in her heart.

"What was the present?" Milo's question stunned her as he waved to the incoming paramedics.

Mr. Garcia shook his head. "If I tell you, it won't be a surprise, son. I figure I got a few months to recreate it. Maybe in time for Christmas."

Milo laughed as he stepped to the side and started talking to the paramedics.

"Your boyfriend is quite the looker." Mrs. Garcia smiled at Quinn.

"He's not my boyfriend." The words tasted like soot as she stared at Milo. He made her feel important. He wrapped her in comfort and had always cheered her on, no matter the places she traveled or the jobs she took. And he'd guided her home. "He's my best friend."

But those words didn't feel right anymore as Quinn wrapped her arms around herself. Milo was her compass, the person who kept her on course.

Mrs. Garcia raised an eyebrow but didn't say anything before hustling off after her husband.

Quinn wasn't needed here anymore. Letting out a sigh, she walked back to her destroyed bungalow. She picked up the photo and smiled at the happy memory before turning her focus to the ruins around her.

It was all really gone. Outside of filing insurance paperwork, this wasn't her home anymore. The one place she'd felt like she could let all her walls down, be herself.

Strong arms wrapped around her, and Quinn leaned back against Milo.

"Ready to go?"

"Are you sure you want me to stay with you, Milo? I'll admit, the idea of walking to St. Brigit's from your apartment is nice." Quinn turned in his arms. She should step back, but she had neither the strength nor the desire to. This was where she felt safe. "But I doubt I will be great company."

"You'll be you. And that is priceless." Milo rested his forehead against hers for a moment. "We'll figure out all the details when we get to the apartment. I actually have a plan I want to run by you."

"A plan?" Quinn let out a soft giggle despite herself. Of course Milo had a plan for what happened if she couldn't come home. "I can't wait to hear it."

"It may be my best plan ever." He smiled, and warmth crept through her belly.

CHAPTER SIX

QUINN'S HAIR WAS WET, and her new tank top clung to her waist as she pulled out the chair at his kitchen island. She smiled as she accepted the glass of wine. Her eyes closed as she took a long sip.

Milo stared at her neck. He wanted to plant kisses there, trail them down her shoulder and lower. Wanted to hold her, to wake up next to her. He wanted so many things.

"So, what is your plan?" Quinn's voice carried through the kitchen.

Her dark eyes called to him. He'd looked at them so often, he knew where each of the gold flecks were.

Quinn called to him.

Her spirit made Milo's soul cry out with need. Her unfailing desire to help, to run from her destroyed home to aid a neighbor… Her ability to pick up and start anew… Everything about her made his heart leap.

"Milo?" Her hand ran along his knee, and he jumped.

"Sorry." Quinn's voice shook. "I... I..." Her eyes raced across his face. "I didn't mean to scare you."

"You didn't." Milo shook his head. "No, you did. But not just now. I mean, I jumped, but..." He shut his mouth. Rambling was not how he'd meant to have this conversation.

"When you kissed me..." Milo bit his tongue. He'd planned this talk and now he was starting in the middle?

"I scared you when I kissed you." Quinn's fingers reached for her wineglass, but she didn't look away.

Milo looked at her and his heart cracked as her bottom lip trembled. His script had flown from his memory. Taking a deep breath, he started again. "I made a mistake." The words were simple, but they were the truth.

"A mistake?" Quinn took another sip of wine before setting her glass down. "Do you want me to leave? I can..."

"No." He reached for her hands. As her fingers wrapped through his, his soul calmed. Quinn grounded him. "I am saying all the wrong things. And I even had a plan."

He gulped and started over.

"When you kissed me..." Quinn looked away, and Milo couldn't stand that. Running a finger along her cheek, Milo waited until she looked at him to continue. "I've dreamed of kissing you for years. Since our undergraduate days. Even before. The time never seemed right to ask, or maybe I was just worried you'd say no. But when it finally happened, my brain went into over-thinking mode. Because—"

Quinn laid a finger against his lips. "Years?"

"Years," Milo confirmed.

Quinn's mouth fell into the cutest O shape.

God, she was adorable.

"I want you. But not for just a night or a few months, Quinn. I've spent the last two days try-ing to figure out how to get you back into my arms. I have a whole plan, but honestly, you've driven it from my mind. All I can think of is kiss-ing you." He leaned forward. "I want to kiss you. Desperately. But if you need time to think—"

Her lips were on his before he could finish.

Quinn…his Quinn.

Pulling her to him, Milo deepened the kiss as the chairs they were sitting in locked together. Quinn in his arms was simply right. Life slowed as he reveled in the taste of her. The feel of her heat pressed against his chest. All of it was in-toxicating.

There was more to discuss, to figure out. But when she was in his arms, none of it seemed to matter. Her fingers traced up his neck and Milo let out a low groan. How had he waited days to have this conversation? Years? Those were days, hours and minutes of kisses he'd thrown away.

"Quinn." Milo let his fingers travel down her sides. "I want you. But if you don't want me to carry you to bed right now, we need to stop."

She pulled back momentarily.

He meant it. If she wanted to take their physical relationship slowly, he'd wait as long as she needed him to.

"I've wanted you since the moment I landed in LA."

The sultry words undid him. There would be time to discuss his plans later. Right now, he needed Quinn.

Sliding from his chair, Milo wrapped his arms around her and lifted her. She let out a light squeal and he kissed her neck. "I've got you, Quinn."

And he was never going to let go.

He dropped kisses on her lips as he carried her to his bedroom. He laid her gently on the bed before reaching for the small lamp. The first time he made love to Quinn was not going to be in the dark.

Her fingers reached for his shirt and he let her pull it off, relishing the desire pooling in her eyes. Had anyone ever looked at him like that? Like they needed him and only him?

Sitting beside her, Milo ran his fingers under her tank top, listening to every tiny change in

her breathing. Cataloging where she responded.
When his fingers finally worked their way to her
breast, Milo's heart raced. He didn't want to rush
this, but his body was taut with need.

Quinn's eyes met his as she lifted her shirt
over her head. She wore no bra. She bit her lips
as she stared at him. "Milo…"

"You are so beautiful," he murmured as he
stared at her. He wanted to know exactly how she
liked to be touched, the noises she made. But he
could see an emotion hovering in her eyes that
he couldn't quite read. "Do you want to stop?"

"No." She kissed his chin.

"Tell me what you're thinking, then." Milo
licked the hollow at the base of her neck, loving
the groan that echoed in the room.

"That this doesn't feel weird." Quinn's hand
trailed along his stomach and down his thigh.
"After so many years of friendship—this feels
right."

"And how, then—" Milo kissed her lips
"—does this feel?" Dipping his head, he sucked
one nipple before turning his attention to the
other.

"Amazing…"

Quinn's voice, was threaded with need, and it
made Milo's own desire pulse more.

She was so beautiful.

Gripping her shoulders, Milo guided her onto
her back. Lowering her shorts, Milo let out a soft

groan. She wasn't wearing any panties. Quinn, his perfect Quinn, was naked on the bed.

"I don't sleep in underwear," Quinn stated as he ran a finger up her thigh.

"That is something I didn't know." Milo held her gaze for a moment before lowering his head. "I love learning new things about you. Like how you taste…"

His senses exploded as he savored her. Her body arched, pushing against him.

This was perfect.

"Milo." He doubted there was a sweeter sound than his name on Quinn's lips when she was in the throes of passion.

He let his fingers trail her calves as he teased her, driving her closer to the edge with his mouth. Her hands running across his shoulders, rolling through his hair, were enough to make him want to bury himself deep inside her. But he was determined not to rush this. They had all night— and all the days after.

"Milo." Quinn gripped his shoulders, and he felt her reach the edge. "Please, Milo. Make love to me."

The plea undid him.

He dropped his jeans to the floor, grabbed a condom from the side table and returned to her.

Quinn's arms wrapped around his neck as she pulled him close. "I need you."

Her mouth captured his as he drove into her.

"Milo!" Her fingers raked his back and he held her tightly.

Nothing in the world mattered more than this moment. This perfect moment. He felt her start to orgasm again and, this time, he didn't hold back. "Quinn."

Her fingers traced his back as he lay in her arms afterward. "That was…" She sighed against his shoulder. "Not sure the words exist." Her voice was lazy with pleasure and exhaustion.

"I agree." He kissed her, his hand caressing her chin. She was so wonderful, and she was here in his arms.

His Quinn.

The sun was rising over LA as Quinn stood in front of the planning boards in Milo's study. He'd outlined his life for the next fifteen years. Something that her parents would have been impressed by. *And* it was impressive—and daunting.

He'd said that he'd worked out a plan for them. But her name was nowhere on any of the lists. So, where did she fit? And did she really want everything planned out? *Controlled?*

She'd lived like that for years. Plans and schedules were one of the things she'd left behind when she'd fled her parents' home. Quinn only planned for her current job and one follow-on assignment. There had been a few times when she hadn't known what was going to happen, yet she'd found that life generally worked out. But she knew Milo needed these.

Lifting the mug of coffee to her lips, she took a deep breath and tried to reorient her mind. She'd spent the night in Milo's bed, though they hadn't slept much. Her body tingled as she remembered the feel of Milo's fingers on her skin. His kisses trailing along her belly. Last night had been lovely. So why was she standing in his study before dawn, unable to quiet the chatter in her mind?

Rolling her neck, Quinn let out a sigh. Milo planned. He thought things through. And he followed through with his plans, no matter what. When he'd decided to resign from the Oceanside Clinic, nothing she or his mom had said had mattered. He was determined.

It was one of the things Quinn loved about him. The word had floated around her last night as he'd held her. Quinn loved Milo. Loved his thoughtfulness, his open heart, his determined spirit. When had her love shifted from that of a cherished friend to romantic?

Did it matter?

Milo had wanted her—had said he'd wanted her for years. But what if she failed to fit into his plans like she'd failed to fit into her parents'?

Her knees trembled. No. Milo was not her parents, and she was not going to imagine the end of this relationship before it even began.

She wasn't.

Quinn forced herself to walk into the kitchen. Placing the mug on the counter, she moved to grab the coffeepot. She poured the coffee then turned to rinse out the pot. Yawning, she reached for her mug, but her fingers didn't quite catch it. The cup tumbled to the floor and she let out a cry. The ceramic shattered at her feet, the sound echoing through the room.

Heat raced along her toes as coffee splashed. "Shoot!" She hopped onto the counter. The coffee spreading across the tiles, clinging to the previously perfect grout.

"In his apartment for less than twenty-four hours and already destroying stuff." Quinn sighed. Somewhere her mother's ghost was saying, *Told you so...*

"I don't care about a mug, Quinn." Milo spoke from the doorway. He wore only boxers, and he looked from the floor to where she was perched on the counter. "Are you okay?"

"Burned my toes, but otherwise fine." Quinn looked around the kitchen. She'd kept towels in the drawer by the sink at the bungalow, and Milo knew where everything was. But she had no idea where he kept his towels.

Because she'd avoided his upscale apartment.

Avoided things that reminded her of her past. But Milo was part of her past, and good. So good. And she was done running.

She was…

Her heart beat with a certainty her brain didn't quite feel, but the rush of emotion was enough to propel her mentally forward. "Where are your towels?"

Milo didn't answer as he started toward her.

"Wait!" Quinn held up her hands. "You're barefoot. The shards…" She didn't want him hurt. And she could see the same emotion wavering on his face. "I promise to stay right here while you get shoes."

He raised an eyebrow as he looked at her. "If you get down, we will have our first fight."

First fight… They were silly words, but they made her smile. She wanted a whole world of firsts with him.

Milo returned quickly. "You're smiling."

"You mentioned our first fight. I am pretty sure that we had our first major fight over your refusal to sit as a subject in my art class in high school."

Milo chuckled as he walked over and pulled two towels from a drawer. He dropped them on top of the mess before lifting her off the counter and carrying her into the other room. "You were mad at me for almost a month. All because I didn't want to pose in a toga."

"It seemed important at the time. Although, if you want to pose for me now…" She kissed the delicate skin behind his ear, enjoying the soft groan that escaped his lips as she slipped down from his arms. Flirting with Milo was fun and easy. But they needed to get the mess she'd made cleaned up, and then discuss what had happened last night.

"I don't think any of the ceramic shards traveled this far." Her fingers tousled his hair as she leaned against his chest.

"I like holding you." Milo sighed. "Though I guess we do need to clean up the mess."

She slipped her flip-flops on and followed Milo back into the kitchen. "I really am sorry. I guess I wasn't too far off when I said I'd make a mess of your place."

"Don't do that." The broken pottery clinked as it hit the bottom of the trash can, but Milo didn't break her gaze.

"Do what?"

He raised an eyebrow before bending to grab the towels from the floor.

Quinn bit her lip. She knew what. He'd gotten on her for years about her self-deprecating jokes. She'd used them to survive in her family, and now her brain just automatically supplied them.

"I know." Quinn shook her head. "My coping mechanism is not the best."

Milo pulled her into his arms and kissed her forehead. "You've had a lot to deal with over the last few days. But you belong here with me. I don't care if you destroy every single mug in the cabinet." He paused for a moment before adding, "Except my favorite mug. It's special."

Milo opened a cabinet and pulled out a slightly misshapen mug.

Her mouth fell open as he held it up for her inspection. "You kept it!" Quinn laughed. The mug was the only thing to survive the twelve weeks of pottery courses she'd taken years ago.

The traveling nursing agency she'd contracted with had mandated the three-month sabbatical after she'd worked in three different disaster zones in nine months. She'd rented a small unit over a pottery studio and taken classes each day—never managing to make more than one lopsided cup.

Drawing and painting were skills that came more or less naturally to her. Her work was pretty, and she'd even sold a few pieces. But no matter what she'd done, the clay refused to turn into anything. The cup was too short, and its handle was misshapen.

"I can't believe you kept that." She'd given it to Milo right after his marriage had ended. He'd held it up and smiled. The first smile she'd seen on his lips for weeks. She'd meant the cup to be a joke, a brief spotlight of happiness before it landed in the trash. But it was in his hands now, being held with such reverence that she thought her heart might explode.

"You worked hard to make this. I remember

you cursing about the 'stupid pottery wheel.'
Very colorful language, if I remember correctly."
Milo put the mug away and then pushed a piece
of hair away from Quinn's eyes. "You can break
everything in this place, Quinn, and it still won't
make me think you don't belong here."

"You never told me your plan." Quinn looked
up and the emotion traveling across Milo's face
made her heart race. "We got distracted." Quinn
grinned. "A few times."

"Yes, we did." Milo dropped his lips to hers.

Quinn's skin tingled as he deepened the kiss.
She'd been in relationships; but this sense of
rightness, of being in the arms of her match,
had never been present. Even during her short
engagement, Quinn had never reacted to James
the way she reacted to Milo. Her body sang every
time he touched her.

"Was your plan to only be distracted a few
times?" She held her breath.

"No." Milo's tone was firm as he stared at her.
"And after last night, if you still think we're better off as just friends, then I have a whole other
plan to make you change your mind."

Her words from the beach felt like another
lifetime ago. And maybe they were. She'd kept
a part of herself locked away in every relationship. Even James had complained that Quinn
never let him all the way in. He'd said that if she
loved him, he wouldn't have to guess what was

going on in her mind. Though *he* hadn't loved *her* enough to stay faithful, to choose her. The wounds across her heart may not bleed anymore, but they'd never fully healed.

But this was Milo, and he already knew so much about her. She could let him into the few places she kept only for herself.

She could.

Grinning, she ran a finger along the outside of his thigh. "I want us to try being us."

"How did you manage to make the word *us* sound so intimate?" Milo's eyes sparked as he pushed another wayward strand of her hair behind her ear.

Milo bent his head, but she stepped back. There was clearly still something she needed to say. "I have two conditions, which I probably should have laid down last night. But you are very good at distractions."

"Name them," Milo stated. "Whatever they are, I'll do it."

"Really?" Quinn raised a brow. If she said she wanted to take a job a few thousand miles from here, what would he say?

No! That was the fear she'd always let worm its way into her brain. *Look for the way you might get hurt, how it might end.* Then she could be prepared. Protected. But she refused to do that with Milo.

"No matter what happens, we stay friends."

Quinn gripped his fingers. "I couldn't stand it if I lost you forever. I want this to work. But if it doesn't..." Her breath caught as Milo pulled her forward.

"I want it to work, too." Milo's lips grazed hers. "But I promise, Quinn. No matter what, I am in your life forever. What's the other condition?"

"You can't plan out everything." Quinn paused as a shadow passed over Milo's eyes. "I don't want to live by an outline, Milo. Let's see where these feelings take us—with no plan."

"No plan?" Milo's voice was tense. "I am not sure I can do that, Quinn. What if I make you a deal?"

She tried to ignore the button of fear in her belly. "What's the deal?"

"I can plan a week at a time—that at least gets us a date night once or twice a week," Milo countered.

"A week at a time..." Quinn nodded. "Deal, but if something fun comes up, we are jumping at it—even if the weekly plan says we're booked."

Milo shook his head before smiling, "Do we settle this with a handshake...or?" Wrapping his arms around her waist, Milo's lips captured hers. "Or would you prefer another action to seal the deal?"

She sighed as he deepened the kiss. If there

was a better way to start the morning than kissing Milo, she didn't wish to find it.

She moved her lips down, kissing the delicate skin along his neck. She loved the way Milo responded to her touch. "Do you want breakfast? Or are you up for more 'distracting'?"

Milo kissed her, his hands wandering to her hips. "I plan to spend most of the day 'distracting' you."

Quinn sighed as his lips trailed to her chest. She kept her gaze off the coffee stain on the kitchen tile. She'd make sure the lingering evidence of her mishap was mopped up later. It wasn't important right now.

CHAPTER SEVEN

THE LAST WEEK had flown by in kisses and a fog of happiness. Quinn smiled as she exited the employee lounge. She couldn't seem to stop smiling.

It was intoxicating and a bit unsettling. Milo raised his head from the end of the hall before heading into a patient's room. The subtle acknowledgment sent a burst of happiness through her.

Glancing at the next patient's chart on her tablet, Quinn frowned. Tara Siemens had checked the "extreme stress" box on the survey they gave to all their patients before their appointments, which didn't make sense to Quinn. Tara was one of her happiest clients.

Many first-time mothers got worried toward the end of their pregnancy. Still, extreme stress could have detrimental effects on the mother and child. Quinn sent an electronic note to Milo, requesting he stop in if he was available. Milo and Dr. Greg had both done additional training on maternal mental health care. It was therefore standard procedure to ask one of them to see any patient who'd checked the extreme stress box.

Quinn opened the door and a sob echoed from the room. "Tara?" Setting aside the tablet, Quinn grabbed the rolling chair and slid in front of her patient.

Her eyes were swollen and red. She wiped at her nose and then took the box of tissues Quinn offered. "So…sorry."

Quinn tapped Tara's knee. "You don't need to apologize. All feelings are allowed in here. What is going on?"

"Brandon." Tara hiccupped and closed her eyes.

Quinn slid her eyes to Tara's hand and noticed her engagement ring was gone. Brandon had attended a few of the appointments with Tara. He'd seemed distracted, but he wasn't the only partner that Quinn had thought was less than enthusiastic about the prospect of parenthood. Most of the time it was nerves, or a coping strategy, particularly in the early days, in case something went wrong. Sometimes, though…

"I am so sorry." Quinn made sure to keep her voice low and soothing. There was never a great time to end an engagement, but when a child was involved, it added a significant amount of stress.

"Want to take a look at your baby?" When a mother was frantic, or concerned, seeing her child often offered a bit of calm. When Tara had checked the stress box on the survey, it had ensured she was placed in one of the rooms with a portable ultrasound machine.

Tara nodded and leaned back on the table. She let Quinn raise her shirt, but silent tears still streamed down her cheeks. "Brandon said he liked the fact that we were so different."

The phrase caught Quinn off guard as she grabbed the gel. She wanted to calm Tara, but relationship discussions were not Quinn's forte—even with the few people she knew well. She made a low noncommittal noise as she dropped a bit of gel against Tara's belly.

"Opposites attract. That was the joke he made when he proposed. He liked my need to order my life, said it balanced his free spirit. Until it didn't…"

The baby's strong heartbeat saved Quinn from trying to find an answer. What was she supposed to say? Opposites sometimes attracted—look at her and Milo. But they'd only just started dating.

"That sounds like a strong heartbeat." Milo's deep voice echoed through the small room. "And you look gorgeous as always, Tara." His voice was soothing as he met Tara's gaze.

"If you like snotty noses and red eyes." Tara sniffled into her tissue.

"Your daughter looks very healthy," Quinn added as Tara stared at the monitor. The monitor that Quinn had hooked up as she'd readied the ultrasound machine showed Tara's heart rate was slowing, too.

Milo caught Quinn's eye, and she carefully rubbed her ring finger. He looked from her hand to Tara's, and she saw recognition flare in Milo's eyes. This wasn't the first time a couple had broken up before the birth of their child, but it was never easy.

"Did you eat breakfast this morning?" Milo asked.

"Egg sandwich," Tara answered.

"Good." Milo nodded. "I had a giant plate of pancakes!"

It was a lie. Milo had eaten a granola bar and a yogurt-to-go, the same as Quinn, as they'd raced out of his place this morning. But he was putting the patient at ease as he asked a series of questions designed to assess her well-being without raising suspicion. Tara's shoulders started to relax as Milo talked to her.

He was gentle but made sure that Tara answered the questions. Pregnancy was a stressful time. Add in trying to find a new place to live and getting over a broken engagement, and you were dealing with issues that could feel overwhelming.

"I think you are going to be just fine," Milo said. "But we are going to give you an emotional check sheet before you leave today. Most people are aware of postpartum depression, but some women will suffer from antepartum depression or depression during pregnancy. Major life changes and the hormone changes going on in your body can make you more susceptible to this kind of depression. And there is nothing wrong with you if it happens."

"Nothing," Quinn reiterated. Many women believed they were supposed to be happy no matter what during their pregnancy. That line of thinking could be dangerous.

Milo nodded. "I need to see to another patient. I enjoyed our chat, Tara."

Quinn talked to Tara about the rain that had started this afternoon and their plans for dinner as they wrapped up the appointment. Easy topics, but Tara didn't cry. That was a good sign.

"You think she'll be okay?" Milo caught Quinn as he exited another patient's room. His thumb rubbed against the back of her wrist.

"I hope so." Quinn quickly straightened the collar of his shirt.

How had he not noticed that?

"She seems so heartbroken."

"Breakups are never easy." Milo flipped through a few screens on his tablet before looking at her.

"She said her ex loved the fact that they were opposites...until he suddenly didn't." Quinn huffed out a breath. It was ridiculous to make comparisons, but she'd always imagined that was how her family had seen her. A perfect, dark-haired opposite to them...until that wasn't good enough.

"Well, that old wisdom that opposites attract is pretty inaccurate."

"It is?" Quinn's heart spun as she stared at him.

If he thought that, what were they doing together?

She picked up and moved when the call came. Milo had moved less than a hundred miles from where they'd grown up. She loved bright, obnoxious decorations and letting life take her where she was supposed to go. Milo liked neutrals and planning everything. He had one-year, three-year, five-year, ten-year and twenty-year plans written on his wall in the study. Quinn didn't even know what three years from now would look like for her—except for the certainty that she wanted Milo in her life.

Milo pushed a piece of hair behind her ear, "I've always thought so. Eventually, the differences drive you apart. Unless the partners can adjust."

"Adjust?" Quinn's skin felt like ice. How was he so casually discussing this? *With her?* Did he not see how different they were? Was the first hint of emotional intoxication overwhelming his rational planning self? And when would he decide that her differences were too much?

"Sure. Everyone adjusts in a relationship. But in an opposites situation, the adjustment has to be larger. I don't know many couples that can overcome that. Though, ideally, you figure that out before starting a family. Plans…" He shrugged. "But life happens." Milo looked at her, his smile gone.

Was she part of life happening? Something that went against Milo's plans? Her mouth was dry as she tried to think of something to say to turn this conversation to something else. Anything else…

"Quinn?" Milo's hand reached for hers. He grasped it briefly before he dropped it. The floor knew that they were dating, but professionalism still needed to be maintained. "I know what you're thinking, but we balance each other. And we have a lot in common. We both love bad movies, hate cooking, love our jobs. We make each other laugh."

But were those enough?

"You're right," Quinn finally murmured, trying to stop the twist of her stomach as it rumbled. "Those pancakes are sounding better by the moment."

Milo raised an eyebrow, but didn't call her out on shifting the topic. "Do you want to do breakfast for dinner? We can make pancakes drizzled with maple syrup, and I am pretty sure that I have some bacon in the fridge. But we could also swing by the market before we go home."

Home. That was a word that struck Quinn. She wanted a home, and Milo including her in the simple statement meant the world to her. But what if their differences set them apart eventually?

"Quinn?" Milo's voice broke her woolgathering.

"Pancakes for dinner would be lovely." The words slipped from her lips without much thought.

"Okay." Milo squeezed her hand one more time before he turned to head to his next patient's room.

Quinn crossed her arms as she watched him go. Milo was right; everyone had to make adjustments in relationships.

They could make it work…couldn't they?

"I'll see you when I get ho—back." Quinn kissed his cheek as she carefully held on to her to-go cup of coffee. She'd purchased the travel mugs the day after she'd spilled the coffee across the kitchen. At least today, she was actually going somewhere with it. No matter how many times Milo told her that he didn't care if she dumped coffee on the floor each morning, she refused to use the ceramic mugs.

It was a silly thing to worry about, but Milo

couldn't press the fear from his throat that Quinn was maintaining a bit of distance. Not much, just a thin veneer around her heart—enough to protect herself. Like she didn't think this was permanent. Like *he* might not be permanent.

This wasn't Quinn's home. Milo understood that. And if her bungalow hadn't been a casualty in the fire, they wouldn't have transitioned to living together so quickly—though he'd probably would've stayed at the bungalow as often as possible.

He enjoyed having her here. Loved waking next to the tangle of dark hair on the pillow beside him. But he hated the fact that Quinn didn't feel completely comfortable in his home. Hated that the gray walls brought forth ghosts better left buried.

With Quinn in residence over the last two weeks, he'd watched her carefully slip into the quiet, palatable Quinn she'd been when living with her parents. Her Quinn shell.

That was the term he'd coined years ago. It had made Quinn laugh, though he knew that she hated that it was necessary to maintain the peace in her home. She'd dropped her defense mechanism once she'd moved out. And he hated that it was currently being used on him—even if she didn't realize she was doing it.

He wanted the real Quinn. The woman who'd bloomed in her own space. Who wore what she wanted, not outfits selected by her mother. The woman who flew wherever was necessary and served everyone. The woman he was in love with.

Love... The word struck him. He'd been dating Quinn a few weeks; that couldn't be right. It was too soon. He'd been with Bianca nearly six months before they'd broached the topic of love.

But as the word settled around him, Milo let it warm him. He loved Quinn. *Loved Quinn.*

He'd never considered theirs a short-term relationship, but as the word rattled around his brain, Milo felt the completion of it. The joy such a simple phrase projected into all the pieces of his soul.

Still, it was too soon to tell her. Quinn had briefly dated a banker in Georgia, and he recalled her breaking it off the minute the guy had hinted at seriousness. She'd said, "Relationships need to be cultivated, not rushed." He was not going to screw this up by moving too fast. Though he wasn't planning to wait too long, either.

Despite her edict to only think one week ahead, his brain had instantly started putting plans together. In another month, it wouldn't seem too rushed if he announced his love. Hopefully, that would give Quinn enough time to realize that they belonged together. If not...? Well, Quinn was worth waiting a lifetime for.

But right now he needed to find a way to make

this place feel more like a home for Quinn. Make her realize that he didn't see it as a temporary space for her. He wanted—*needed*—her to want to stay in Los Angeles. With him.

Particularly since Miranda had decided to interview the senior OB from Valley General. Milo had quietly reached out to a colleague in the unit and inquired about potential openings. They'd told him that they expected an opening in the next few months, which suggested that Dr. Torres was planning to leave, even if she didn't get the position at St. Brigit's. All Milo's plans were falling into place; he just had to make sure Quinn wanted to stay.

Crossing his arms, Milo stared at the kitchen. An idea flew into his mind. And with Quinn on a ten-hour shift, he had just enough time to pull it off.

Picking up the phone, he dialed his sister's number.

"It's not even eight, Milo! Some of us start our mornings a little later." Gina yawned, but she didn't hang up.

"I need paint. Bright yellow paint and sunflower pictures." His fingers itched to get to work. To make the feelings bursting through his heart erupt onto the walls.

"You are calling before eight to talk about redecorating. I thought you wanted all calming tones in your place. Yellow—"

"Is bright and fun. *And* Quinn's favorite color." Milo smiled as he stared at the kitchen walls. The bungalow was gone, but he could bring a bit of it here for her. His chest swelled as he mentally ran through the checklist. This was perfect, and Quinn was going to love it.

"Quinn." His sister sounded much more awake now. "I'll make some calls."

"I'm headed to the hardware store. You know where the key is." Milo grinned as he said a quick goodbye. He loved Quinn, and this was going to make her smile.

Quinn belonged in a yellow kitchen with bright pictures. And she belonged with him.

Quinn flexed her shoulders, glad her shift had finally ended. She'd overseen two deliveries that had begun long before her ten-hour stint had started. Both mothers were fine, but they'd labored for more than twenty hours and were exhausted, as was the staff. And she'd wished Milo had been there to help.

It was silly to miss him when she'd seen him just this morning. She'd known a few people who claimed working with their significant other was stressful, but working with Milo was invigorating. He challenged and supported her.

Her stomach grumbled. The two deliveries had kept her from being able to run out to the food trucks that always parked across from the medical park that housed St. Brigit's, and the few items of questionable sustenance she'd procured from the vending machine had not staved off hunger for long.

Her belly growled again, and the gentleman on the other side of the elevator car looked at her. So many people didn't realize that hospital employees rarely got full lunch or dinner breaks. This wasn't the first time she'd come home with an empty stomach. But it was nothing that a sandwich and a hot shower couldn't fix.

The door to the apartment opened as she stepped out of the elevator. Milo leaned against the door frame, exhaustion coating his eyes, too.

"Are you okay?" Quinn asked as she kissed his cheek. "And how did you time opening the door for me when I got off the elevator?"

"I'm great." Milo dipped his lips to hers just as his stomach rumbled. "A little hungry. I lost track of time and missed lunch. And I asked Jamison to let me know when you got here."

"You asked the doorman to look out for me?" Quinn smiled. "What did you get up to today?" Her stomach growled again. "And please tell me it involved cooking dinner."

"It didn't." Milo grinned. "But the pizza and beer I ordered were delivered ten minutes ago."

"Bless you." As Milo moved aside, Quinn

stepped into the apartment and stopped. Her purse slipped from her fingers, landing with a thud.

She covered her heart with her hands as she stared at the bright yellow kitchen and the sunflower pictures hanging above the sink. It was the exact same color as her kitchen at the bungalow. Her pictures had been ones she'd painted, but these were wonderful, too.

All thoughts of her grumbling stomach flew from her mind as she looked at the happy kitchen.

This *gesture was...*

Her brain couldn't find the right word. It was the most thoughtful thing that anyone had ever done for her.

Turning, she stared at Milo. "You painted the kitchen." Her lip trembled as she looked at him. How did she thank him for this? It was too much and so perfect.

His smile was huge as he stepped closer to her and wrapped an arm around her waist. His lips brushed her lips as if he couldn't stand another minute of being apart, either.

Running her free hand over the countertop, she gazed at his hard work. He'd spent the entire day doing this—*for her.* "How did you manage to paint and decorate this all in one day?"

Milo dragged a hand through his hair as he looked at her. "I had a bit of help. I called my sister, and she found the drawings for me. Gina used a few of her designer connections and had them delivered while I was painting." Milo opened the cabinet. "She even found some of those sunflower mugs that you had." He paused. "I know it's not quite the same—"

Quinn kissed him. It wasn't her bungalow—it was better. It was a gift. The most perfect gift. Happiness raced through her, a delirious sensation after a long day. She deepened the kiss, enjoying the low moans echoing in Milo's throat.

He pulled back and gave her a warm smile. "I'm glad you like it. Maybe we should paint the bedroom, too."

She laughed as he held her close. How could she not love it? "Blue and green can be very relaxing."

Milo traced kisses along her jaw before capturing her mouth.

She could melt into him, sink into the wonderful feelings racing through her. Quinn threaded her fingers through his hair. "Thank you."

He dipped his head to her neck. "I need to hop in the shower before I eat. You don't have to wait for me. I won't be long."

"Or I could join you." Quinn laughed as he grabbed her hand and headed for the bathroom.

"This is one room that I wouldn't change a single thing about." Quinn sighed as she watched Milo lean in to turn on the shower. His backside was a work of art.

She licked her lips as she slid her hands down his tight butt before unbuttoning the top of his jeans. She unzipped his pants and loved the shift in his breathing—loved knowing that she turned him on so easily. Quinn stared at him as she pulled his pants off and stroked him.

Milo's fingers grazed her stomach as he tugged her T-shirt off. Her bra dropped to the floor next. "If you want to focus on a shower, you need to step into it—now." His voice was deep as he ripped his shirt over his head.

"And if I don't want to?" Quinn smiled as she kissed him and then slowly trailed her mouth down his magnificent body.

"Quinn..." Milo's moan sent goose bumps across her skin. She enjoyed nothing more than the sound of her name on his lips as she turned him on.

She kissed her way along his thighs, coming close to his manhood, but then moving away each time. Quinn smiled as Milo's large hands cupped her head.

"Quinn, love..."

She took him in her mouth then, loving the control. She gripped his butt and sighed at the sounds of pleasure echoing through him. He pulled her up and kissed her.

"God, Quinn." Milo shuddered as he sat her on the counter. "You are too amazing."

"Imagine if you'd let me finish." Quinn was surprised by the boldness in her voice. She had never been a bold lover, but with Milo, everything felt so easy.

Milo kissed the tender spot below her ear he'd found their first night together. "I have every plan to finish," he vowed, his thumb pressing against her nub as he watched her. Milo took one of her nipples between his lips as he continued to use his fingers to drive her closer to the edge.

"Milo…" Quinn's body moved against his. The way he was teasing her felt glorious, but it wasn't enough. She needed him. All of him… now.

"Milo," she repeated.

His tongue flicked her nipple, and her body erupted. "Want something?" His eyes dilated with pleasure as he met her gaze. "All you have to do is ask. I'll give you anything, Quinn. Anything."

"I need you." Quinn ran her hand down his length. "Now!"

Milo grabbed a condom from the drawer and sheathed himself quickly. Pressing against her, he captured her lips. He put one hand around her waist and pressed the other to the mirror as he buried himself deep inside her.

Quinn gripped his shoulders, completely lost to the oblivion that was she and Milo.

* * *

"There's a new patient asking for you," Sherrie said, nodding to room six.

Quinn looked toward the room, then back at Sherrie. Patients often asked for specific midwives, but St. Brigit's had a rule that all midwives and OBs saw all patients because when a woman went into labor, a particular midwife or doctor might not be on call.

"A new patient?" Quinn looked at Sherrie. "Why is she asking for me?"

Sherrie shrugged. "Not sure. But her husband asked if they could speak to you before they left. I can always have Heather tell them you aren't available when she goes in to schedule their next appointment. But figured if you had a moment, I'd pass along the request."

"I have a moment." Quinn smiled. Maybe a friend from overseas had moved into the local area. More likely, one of her former patients had recommended St. Brigit's because of working with Quinn.

She opened the door and froze. A woman with curly dark hair was sitting on the edge of the exam table, a brilliant smile on her face. But it was the presence of the man in the room that kept her feet planted at the entryway.

"Quinn." Her brother's voice faltered a bit, but his eyes were soft as they met hers. "It's good to see you."

"Asher." Quinn stepped into the room and shut the door. Her chest was tight, as if she couldn't get enough oxygen. He'd been a teenager when their parents had cut contact with Quinn. She'd briefly hoped they might reconnect after Asher had divided their parents' estate, but her phone calls and texts had gone unanswered. She'd looked him up on social media a few times since, though not recently. But she'd never reached out—it was clear from his silence that he hadn't been interested in having a relationship with her.

What was he doing *here*? *Having a baby.*

They'd never been close, not even as children. She couldn't remember them playing together more than a handful of times. It could have been a survival technique. Since her parents' focus had always been on what she did wrong, Asher had had a bit more freedom. Now that he was here, all that distance didn't seem to matter so much.

He had a brilliant smile as he looked from Quinn to the woman on the table. "This is Samantha." Asher gestured to the woman before gripping her hand. She wasn't visibly pregnant, but St. Brigit's typically started seeing patients around the ten-week mark. "My wife," Asher added, beaming as he looked at her.

"Congratulations," Quinn murmured. She meant the words. No matter what, she would always want the best for her brother. And she couldn't remember ever seeing him smile like this. It made her smile, too.

"I couldn't find your address or phone number when we were sending out invitations. It was a tiny ceremony, about two years ago." Asher rubbed the back of his head. "Family stuff has never been my strong suit." His jaw hardened as he squeezed his wife's hand. "Though I'm learning."

They'd hardly had good role models to follow. "It is good to see you, Asher. And to meet you, Samantha." The moment was awkward, but how could any moment with a sibling be normal after so many years of no contact?

He swallowed. "I know this isn't the time or place for a reunion. But I saw your picture on the wall in the waiting room and I couldn't believe it." Asher shrugged. "I thought you were overseas. I checked a few times online. Even started a letter to you once, but I didn't know what to write."

So she hadn't been the only one unsure how to reach out. Pushing through the discomfort, Quinn smiled. "I was. But I've been back for almost a year. It is good to see you, Asher, but I can't treat your wife. Not as a family member." Quinn looked at Samantha. "Not that I wouldn't like to…"

The door to the room opened and Milo stepped

in. His fingers pressed briefly against her back as he said, "Asher." His tone was polite but firm.

"Milo." Asher nodded at him. "I must have been too focused on Quinn's picture to notice you worked here, too. This is my wife, Samantha."

Samantha waved. "It's nice to meet both of you, but we've probably taken up enough of your workday."

Samantha was right, but Quinn didn't want to waste the opportunity. She grabbed a paper towel, and wrote down her number. "Just in case."

Asher smiled as he stared at the number. "I'll text you. It was really good to see you, Quinn."

"You, too, Asher, and nice to meet you, Samantha. Your midwife will be in to see you in just a moment."

Once outside the exam room, Quinn leaned against the closed door for a minute before she looked at Milo. "Running to my rescue?"

"Yes." Milo dropped a quick kiss on the top of her head. "Though you seemed to have it under control."

"My heart is racing, and my brain still hasn't fully figured out what is going on. So much has happened so quickly."

Her hands were shaking, but she felt good. Surprisingly good. "I think I'm fine. Guess I'm going to be an aunt! Though I'm not sure how much Asher will want me to be involved. Probably not much."

"Or maybe he would love for his children to get to know their beautiful, smart, fun aunt Quinn. He didn't tell Samantha they should cancel their appointment and run when he saw your picture. Focus on the potential good outcome. At least for now."

Milo offered her a quick hug before rushing off down the hall to his next appointment.

So much had happened in the last month and a half, Quinn was realizing that LA could be just as much of an adventure as any of the places she'd worked before. Her skills were just as useful here as they'd been anywhere else. She smiled as she watched Milo duck into another patient's room. Her heart had been right to pull her here. Despite the fire, the sweet definitely outweighed the sour.

"Did he call?" Milo knew the answer as Quinn looked away from the phone and plastered on a fake smile. If Milo could thrash Asher, he would. "I'm sorry, Quinn."

What was wrong with her family? Why couldn't they see the incredible woman she was?

"It's fine." Her voice was tired as she slid down beside him on the couch. Her shoulders sagged. "At least he sent me his number. Maybe asking if he wanted to grab dinner was too much." Her lip trembled as she flipped her phone over. "No one ever wants to keep me."

The final phrase was so quiet Milo didn't know if Quinn realized she'd said it aloud. But it ripped through him.

How could she think that?

Her family, and that lout James, may have thrown away one of the best things to happen to them, but so many others hadn't. "That is *not* true," he whispered as he kissed her forehead.

Milo sat up and pulled her hands into his lap. He waited until she looked at him. "I have always kept you. Ever since you started that food fight, it's been you and me."

"Pretty sure *you* started that food fight." She smiled, but it didn't quite reach her eyes.

"I'm not the only one, either." Milo kissed the tip of her nose. Her parents' desire to make her into something she wasn't, to force her into their mold and then withhold love when she didn't meet their impossible standards and routines, bordered on evil, in Milo's opinion. Especially because they'd doted on Asher. They had been capable of being loving parents and yet had chosen not to be with Quinn.

"Thanks, Milo." She kissed his cheek. "I shouldn't have said it, and certainly not to you. You're always there for me."

But her voice wasn't steady and the tears he saw her trying to hide nearly broke him. She didn't see herself the way others saw her, and that ended tonight.

"Your phone has the number for the head of Doctors Without Borders, right?"

"Yes, because I worked a few missions for them." Quinn shrugged.

"No. Julio has your number because you bonded late one night in some out-of-the-way place while he was still just one of their regular physicians. He calls you to ask your opinion because of how impressed he was with you." Milo paused. "And what about the hospital in Boston that has twice offered you a position as a senior midwife in their unit? And that's just in your professional life...

"There have been cards arriving here for the last two weeks from your friends around the world sorry to hear that your bungalow burned. Not to mention the box of clothes and photos that arrived yesterday, from someone named Christine, to replace some of what you lost."

Quinn's lips captured his, and Milo held her for a minute before pulling away. "Trying to silence me with kisses?"

Her lips tipped up as her dark eyes held his. "Maybe." Quinn leaned her head back. "It's uncomfortable to hear so many good things about myself."

Particularly when you grew up hearing so many bad things.

Quinn left those words unstated, but Milo knew she was thinking them. "If Asher doesn't want a relationship with you, that is *his* loss." Milo kissed the top of her head.

"I know." Quinn leaned against him. "I really do know that—objectively." She was silent for a minute before adding, "But he's my family, and it just hurts."

Rubbing her arm, Milo held her close. He'd grown up in a loving family. They'd supported him and never made him feel like he was anything other than a beloved son. He'd never felt like his mom loved him more or less than his sister. In his mother's eyes, they were equal.

"I'm here for you," Milo added, hoping it was enough.

"Thank you." Quinn sat up and smiled. "I lo—"

Her cell interrupted her, and Milo glared at it. What if Quinn was going to say I love you? But if Asher had interrupted... Well, it would be worth it to make Quinn happy. Though he'd give the man a hard time about it at some point.

Quinn answered, and he saw her eyebrows twitch before she smiled. It wasn't the giant smile that always sent such a thrill down his body, so it probably wasn't Asher. At least someone else had brightened her mood. She kissed his cheek and then stood up, walking into the kitchen as she continued the call.

"Florida?" Quinn laughed before looking over at him.

Florida? Milo's mind spun into overdrive. This was the call that he'd been terrified of since they'd started dating. She'd made connections all over the world—literally. It had always been only a matter of time before her phone rang again with news of a new opportunity, a new adventure.

Milo hadn't been kidding when he'd spoken about how many people wanted to work with Quinn. Even if her family had been unable to see the wonderful woman she was, her colleagues admired her greatly.

"I'll think about it."

Those words sent a splash of pain racing through him. Florida was on the other side of the country. An all-day plane trip away from him. His stomach knotted as she grinned and put her phone in her pocket.

"How do you feel about the Atlantic Ocean?" Quinn asked, handing him a beer.

"I've never really thought about it." That wasn't completely true. He'd rolled the idea of living and working somewhere else around his brain a few times since they'd started dating. He'd even stood in front of his wall of plans a few days ago. But the image of his father's face and his hand pointing to the nameplate kept floating in Milo's mind—a beacon that stayed his hand whenever he picked up the eraser, thinking about changing his plan.

"But I like California." That was true. He'd always felt his path was here, even as he watched Quinn plot her course around the world.

Quinn held up a finger. "Don't worry. I'm not actually planning on taking this position."

His heart lifted with joy before crashing. *This position.* She hadn't said that she wouldn't consider moving at all. His gaze flew to the yellow kitchen, and he racked his brain, trying to think of a way he could compete with the likely possibility that an offer would come that she would want to take.

"Why?" He hated the selfish thoughts running through his mind. But that didn't stop his need to know the answer.

Quinn paused as she looked at him. She opened her mouth, but closed it a second later. Then she shrugged. "Because I like where I'm at right now."

That wasn't what she'd thought about saying; he was nearly certain. Milo's heart yearned to hear what had been on the tip of her tongue before she'd swallowed it. He should be happy, thrilled, but the words *right now* pounded in his brain.

Quinn's gaze wandered to the window behind him. "But I have always wanted to run my own unit…"

"Is that what the job is? Does that mean you *are* thinking about it?" Milo tried to gauge the look in her eyes. She almost looked like she was trying to talk herself out of it.

"No, I'm not considering it. But thinking about running my own unit makes me smile." Quinn tapped his knee. Her voice was bright, but he could hear the bit of longing in it. "But I'm not moving to Florida. So, you don't need to worry about it. Florida's not high on my list of places I want to work."

List of places?

His throat constricted as he looked at her. How long was that list? His brain was spinning as he tried to focus.

"But you said you'd think about it?" Milo knew he shouldn't press, but there was something about the glint in her eye when she'd mentioned running her own unit. The head of St. Brigit's had at least another ten years before she retired. That was a long time to wait. If Quinn really wanted to run her own unit soon—it wouldn't be here.

"Terri is persistent!" Quinn laughed. "If I'd said no right away, he'd say I hadn't thought it through and my inbox would be full of emails detailing the wonders of Orlando. I bet he'd even offer Disney World tickets."

"Anaheim is less than thirty miles from here.

We can see Mickey anytime." Milo hated the defensiveness in his tone.

"When did you become such a Disney fan?" Quinn smiled as she set her beer down. "I seem to remember you complaining about the ticket prices, parking and lines when we went as teenagers. It was a very grown-up complaint, if memory serves." Her lips pressed against his cheek as her fingers tracked his thigh.

"The lines *were* long, and it *was* hot. But we still had a great time." Milo had taken her for their sixteenth birthdays, excited to be able to drive them there himself. For a moment that day, he'd considered kissing her. He'd looked at Quinn and wondered what if…? But the moment had passed.

But she was here now. Her fingers slid up to the waistband of his jeans, and the memory flew from his brain. "You're trying to distract me," Milo murmured as Quinn placed light kisses along his jawline.

"There is nothing more to discuss. I'm not interested in the Orlando job. What I am interested in…" Her fingers slid inside his pants, and Milo lost his ability to reason. There would be plenty of time to work out a plan.

Plenty of time.

CHAPTER EIGHT

"QUINN!" OPAL CALLED from the registration desk. "Can you do a quick review of this transfer chart?"

"Sure." Quinn took the tablet from Opal's outstretched hand. It was unusual for a patient to transfer their care from St. Brigit's, but sometimes the facility wasn't a good fit. Or, if the pregnancy was high risk, they'd recommend delivering at a nearby hospital instead. But before they transferred a patient's records, a midwife or OB had to do a quick review of the chart to make sure everything was in order.

Her stomach shook as she stared at the name on the chart: Samantha Davis. "I can't do the review." Even if it wasn't against policy for her to review her brother's wife's chart, Quinn couldn't have stomached it. Why had Asher asked to see her if he was just going to ghost her again?

Pain trickled across her skin. She knew it wouldn't be visible to anyone, but her whole body ached at th...th...the... Her heart screamed *betrayal*, but her mind refused to accept the word. *Denial.*

Asher had never spoken up on her behalf. Never interjected to support her as she'd argued that she didn't want to do the activities her parents thought were best, even though she'd seen him roll his eyes at her mother's daily schedules, too. She could forgive him for not realizing how differently their parents treated them when they were children—no child should think their parents capable of only loving one of their children—but the inequity in their family had been so glaring, he had to have seen it as a teenager and as a young adult. And yet he'd said nothing; he'd just accepted it.

She couldn't have treated his wife. As a family member, the relationship was too personal.

Even for a family that never spoke.

But apparently just being in the same facility as Quinn was too much. The hurt spun through her as she stared at her brother's name on the forms. They had the same last name, had lived in the same house for sixteen years, but that hadn't been enough to bind them.

"Quinn?" Opal's question drew her back to reality. "Are you okay?"

No. She was going to lose it, and she couldn't do that here. Not now. "Yes, but Samantha Davis is my brother's wife. So, you will need one of the other midwives or doctors to review this before the transfer." She was impressed that her voice didn't break, even as a piece of her spirit shattered.

"Ah-hh." Opal's eyes widened. "I didn't know you had a brother."

Why wouldn't your brother want his wife to deliver here? That was the question hovering in Opal's eyes, but Quinn knew she wouldn't ask it. At least, not to Quinn. This was going to be fodder for gossip, but what answer could Quinn give?

"Oh, Dr. Russell." Opal's eyes brightened as Milo joined them. "Since you're here, can you do a quick patient review for me?"

Milo's gaze slid to Quinn. She saw the recognition flash across his face as he made the logical leap to why she wasn't the one reviewing the records.

Milo knew Asher hadn't returned her invitation to dinner. Hadn't even texted a polite "too busy." He knew it hurt, even if Quinn tried to pretend that it didn't. His hand brushed her back as he leaned over to take the tablet. It was a small motion, one that no one else would notice, but it sent a flood of comfort through her, and her heart clung to it.

He'd been a bit odd after Terri had called to offer her the job in Orlando, though she'd tried her best to quiet his fears. Before coming back to California, Quinn would have jumped at the offer—the adventure of running her own unit.

But moving didn't hold the appeal it once had. Milo's closeness settled her. From the moment she'd arrived at LAX, the pull of the road had relaxed. The driving need to move, to find a new place—her place—had almost vanished.

Her place was here.

That probably would have terrified her if it wasn't for Milo. Maybe his need to control life's chaos really did balance her need to be propelled by her emotions and gut instinct.

The idea of running her own unit was appealing, but another opening would present itself eventually. That was one lesson she'd learned. Life had a habit of providing opportunities that surprised you. Maybe not always with happiness and joy, but those things would be mixed in, too.

"Molly is in room two for a postpartum follow-up." The nurse's aide's voice was taut as she walked toward them, looking from Quinn to Milo. "She checked off three items on her postpartum depression survey, and she's trying to hold back tears."

"Okay." Quinn took the tablet and headed toward room two. At least this gave her something to focus on. More than fifteen percent of women suffered from postpartum depression, but many still felt there was shame in admitting it.

In Quinn's experience, if a recently delivered

mother was acknowledging there was a problem, that was a win. But if they checked more than two boxes, they were also probably experiencing additional symptoms.

"Molly." Quinn smiled as she walked into the room. Her son was asleep in his carrier and Molly was chewing on a fingernail. "How are you feeling?"

"Fine!" Molly's response was too bright. Her hair was unkempt, and there were bags under her eyes and spit-up on her clothes. All symptoms of having a newborn at home. But the watery eyes, anxious glances at her son and nail biting sent a bead of worry through Quinn.

"It's okay if you're not."

Molly's eyes darted between Quinn and the door.

"What's going on?"

She tapped her chewed fingernails against her knees before letting out a sigh that was nearly a sob. "I wanted to be a mother for so long." Molly's lips shook. "Then we adopted Owen. It was amazing. *Is amazing.* But when we found out I was pregnant…" Molly closed her eyes and hugged herself tightly. "It felt like I was going to get to experience something I missed with Owen." Molly hiccupped and wiped a tear away.

"If I can't be happy now, what kind of mom does that make me?" Molly looked at Quinn, and the dam of emotions broke. Tears cascaded down her cheeks, and she sucked in a breath.

"It makes you a mom who is dealing with the stress of having two children and a body that's been through a trial, because birth is hard. There's a reason we call it labor!" Quinn patted Molly's knee. "This is not uncommon. It isn't."

"I want to run away when Adam cries." Molly's cheeks flamed as she told the dark secret. "I never felt that way with Owen. And Owen is clingy, which I know is to be expected with the new baby. But after what feels like marathon breastfeeding sessions with Adam, snuggling with Owen is too much. That isn't how a good mom responds."

"Yes. It is, sometimes." Quinn looked at Molly. "This is postpartum depression, and you cannot just force it away. There is no shame in saying it. You're very brave for telling me these things."

"Owen is into everything, and I am trying to make sure he doesn't feel left out, but Adam is up all the time, and breastfeeding hasn't been super easy. My mother took Owen last weekend to give us a bit of a break. It's easier with one." Molly let out an uncomfortable laugh as she stared at her son.

That statement cut at Quinn's heart. She'd heard the same from countless mothers. The fact that her own mother had only wanted one, and would have liked to return her adopted daughter, didn't have any bearing on what was going on with Molly.

"I bet it was," Quinn agreed and nodded when Molly's mouth gaped.

"I'm terrible." Molly wiped a tear away.

"No, you're not." Quinn kept her voice level but firm. "There is nothing wrong with the truth, Molly. You've gone from having a wonderful, lovely toddler—who, by your own description, is into everything—and added a newborn to the mix. And your body is still healing. How did you feel when Owen was gone?"

"A little more relaxed. But I missed him terribly. He only stayed one night before I asked Mom to bring him home." She ran the tissue under her nose and then sighed. "I can't stop crying, and I feel like a failure."

Reassuringly, Quinn tapped Molly's hand. "You are a good mother. Do you know how I know?"

Molly shook her head, but didn't answer.

"Because you love your children. That is what matters. It's what they…" Quinn swallowed the lump that had unexpectedly materialized in her throat. "It's what they remember most—the love."

Especially if it isn't given.

But she left that last thought unstated.

"Now, let's get *you* taken care of."

* * *

"Are you okay?"

Milo's question hit her as she stared at the charred hill in the distance. She didn't have an easy answer. How had it been less than two months since she'd sat and avoided looking out this window while her home burned? And how had so much changed?

"I don't know." The truth slipped through Quinn's lips. After discovering that Asher and his wife had transferred their care, and dealing with the emotions of Molly's postpartum issues, Quinn felt drained. Her tank was empty.

Milo's arms wrapped around her, and Quinn sighed but didn't step away. "We're at work."

"And you've had a long day," Milo kissed the top of her head as he released her. "I am sorry about Asher."

"It's not just him." Quinn hugged herself.

"Is it the Orlando job?" Milo's voice was tight.

"What?" Quinn frowned. This was the fourth time he'd brought it up over the last three days. Why would he not drop it? She'd sent a polite refusal to Terri this morning. Though he'd sent back the standard request to give it one more thought, Quinn knew Terri wouldn't press. "No, it's that Molly has postpartum depression. She made some comments about it being easier with only one kid. She loves her children, and with medication and the support group Sherrie set up several years ago, she is going to be fine. But with Asher's refusal to contact me and her having an older adopted son, my brain is just spinning."

"That's to be expected," Milo stated. "The last two months would have overloaded anyone. It doesn't make you weak for being tired—and maybe even a little furious at the universe."

She shook her head as he offered her a lopsided smile. "Maybe I need to get away." She looked at the hills and sighed. A small holiday would be nice, and they both had a healthy amount of vacation days stocked up.

"Away?" Milo's voice caught as he looked at her.

"Sure, running away—" The unit alarm interrupted her. She looked at Milo. "Who is in labor?"

"No one," Milo called as he raced for the door.

Was there no time for anyone to breathe?

Maybe it was too soon, but they were going to take a vacation together. Maybe she could convince Milo to throw a dart on a map and just go.

"It's time to push," Milo ordered as Tien gripped Quinn's hand. The woman had labored at home for almost nine hours and she'd been eight centimeters when she'd walked in. Her husband had boarded a plane on the east coast as soon as he could once her labor started, but he was still at least two hours out. Milo understood why she was so distraught, but babies waited for no one.

"My husband isn't here." Tien let out a wail as Quinn helped her get into position. She'd repeated that line every few minutes since arriving. Probably hoping that the mantra would either speed up his arrival or delay the baby's.

"I know." Quinn's voice was soft as she held Tien's gaze. "I know he wants to be here, too."

That was true. Milo had served as Tien's primary OB over the last nine months. Her husband had been to every appointment but the last one, when his job had sent him to DC for a week, but he'd video-called. Tien had still had four weeks before her due date—but babies rarely adhered to scheduled dates, unfortunately. If Milo had been a betting man, he'd have bet that Tien had at least two more weeks before delivering her first child.

Quinn pressed a cloth to Tien's forehead. "Your son or daughter is going to be here soon. And then you'll get to introduce your new child to your husband when he arrives." Quinn took a deep breath. "But right now, it's time for you to do your job. Dr. Russell and I are here for you."

Her voice was the perfect mix of comforting and authoritative. Tien let out a small cry as she sat up.

Milo nodded to Quinn. She was impressive. Even after the long day, and the shock of learning that Asher's wife had requested to transfer her care, Quinn was taking care of another mother. With no hint of the turmoil that Milo knew she must be experiencing.

"All right, Tien. Push!" Milo ordered.

Milo found Quinn cooing over Tien's tiny daughter as she sat with the new mother. They'd been off the clock for almost two hours, but traffic from LAX was so bad that Tien's husband still hadn't made it to the hospital. So, she'd stayed at St. Brigit's to keep her company while Milo ran home to get some dinner ready.

He'd done his best to make sure everything at home would be just right when he finally managed to get Quinn to leave St. Brigit's. Her quip about running away was still sending chills through him. After the day she'd had—hell, the last several weeks she'd had—he could understand the sentiment, but it still frightened him.

They both needed a hot meal and a full night of sleep. Quinn should be dead on her feet after the day's emotional roller-coaster ride, but you would never be able to guess it from the happy laughs coming from Tien's room. How was he so lucky to have found such a terrific partner?

Milo's heart ached as he watched Quinn take

the little girl from Tien. She cuddled the baby, and he saw her shoulders relax just a bit. She'd discussed children a few times over the years. Always wistfully, like she didn't know if she'd ever get the chance.

But staring at Quinn with a child in her arms, Milo felt the future tug at him. She'd be an excellent mother. She'd fight for her children and make sure they never doubted her love.

And he wanted to be the one standing next to her through all of it. Wanted to plan a life that included family and fun, and endless happy memories.

"Dr. Russell!" Tien's husband, Jack, ran toward him with a man who was nearly his mirror image. "Where's Tien?"

"Deep breaths, son," the other man said.

"Room five." Milo nodded toward the doorway.

"Thank you." Jack's father grinned as he watched his son run into the room. "The nurse at the front desk told him the same thing, but I'm not sure his brain fully heard it in his rush."

"Understandable." Milo nodded to Quinn as she exited the room and gestured to the employee lounge before heading to grab her things.

Jack's father leaned over and peered through the door. "I can't wait to meet my granddaughter, but I think my son and daughter-in-law deserve a few minutes before Papa intrudes." The pride radiating off the man was intoxicating. "Not sure there's a better moment than seeing your son hold his own child."

The words hung in the space around Milo, pushing at him as he watched Jack's father wipe a tear from his eye and turned to go meet his new granddaughter. This was a moment Milo's father had never had—and would never get. The small ache that never left him throbbed and a wave of unexpected grief passed over him.

For a moment, Milo was a kid again. Reaching for his dad. But the memory was foggy, like so many of them were. And his voice refused to come to Milo.

Quinn's hand was warm as it slipped into his. "What's wrong?"

The quiet words drew him back to the present, and her presence grounded him. How did you explain that you'd lost your dad's memory? That it was easier to draw his face to your mind only after you looked at his picture? That you felt like a failure for not keeping his memory closer?

The right words didn't appear, and Milo wasn't certain he was strong enough to utter them if they did.

"Long day." He threw his arm around Quinn's shoulders. "But it's nothing a plate of hot food, a shower, and a night in your arms won't fix."

She raised an eyebrow, and Milo could see her

desire to call out the lie. Instead, she patted his chest just over his heart and kissed his cheek. "Let's go home."

Quinn was curled on the couch reading when Milo's phone buzzed. He'd been in his study for most of the afternoon. He'd said he was catching up on paperwork, but the two times that Quinn had peered in the door, he'd been staring at his planning boards. She'd asked if he needed any help, but he'd just kissed her and told her he was fine.

Ever since coming home after Tien's birth, Milo had been… Her brain searched for the right word. *Reflective.*

If she asked, he said it was nothing, but she knew that wasn't true. Something was bothering him, and he hadn't told Quinn what it was. It felt like he was actively keeping it from her.

Milo had maintained his planning boards for as long as Quinn had known him. They gave him a sense of peace, of control. He only adjusted them when he was certain of the plan he wanted to follow.

And her name hadn't appeared anywhere on them.

It was selfish to want it when she'd ordered him not to plan out their relationship. Told him not to focus too far into the future. But she was surprised by how much she wanted the confirmation that he saw her there, wanted the security of knowing what five years from now looked like. It was terrifying for a woman who'd spent the last decade carefully avoiding any sort of long-term plan. Yet she couldn't force the desire away.

When the phone buzzed again, she pushed away the prickle of panic as she answered. "Hi, Diana. Milo is in his study doing…" Quinn hesitated. She had no idea what was keeping him so long. "Something," she finished lamely.

Milo's mother let out a soft laugh. "Knowing my son, he's probably planning something. Or adjusting a plan, or thinking about adjusting a plan."

Quinn chuckled, too, but the sound was false, even to her own ears. She was certain that was what Milo was up to, and part of her wanted to ask what changes he was making. Most important, if they included her,

They'd moved in together before they'd even officially started dating. They were happy. *They were!* But occasionally he looked at her and she could see the doubt hovering in his eyes. And it had been there several times since she'd been offered the job in Florida.

Was he waiting for her to leave?

Pushing the thought to the side, Quinn stood up and wandered to the kitchen. "I suspect you're right about the plans. It's his favorite hobby."

"Yes," his mother stated, an underlying note to the word that Quinn couldn't place.

"Is there something I can do for you?"

"Felix and I are having a barbecue this weekend. We usually try to plan these things out. Otherwise, Milo or Gina—or both—are busy. But the weather is going to be so nice."

There was something she wasn't saying… Quinn was almost certain, but then she shook herself. Now she was looking for things to worry about with Milo's mom? She needed to get control of herself. "We aren't on call this weekend. What should I bring?"

"How about some dessert? Gina's already promised the dip—which I know Milo hates."

Quinn laughed. "Well, dessert is easy enough."

"Wonderful!" She could hear Diana's smile through the phone. "I can't wait to see you, Quinn—and Milo, too."

Diana had been thrilled when they'd told her they were dating. Quinn had always felt comfortable around his mother and sister, but they were really making her feel like part of the family.

An important part, not just Milo's girlfriend.

"Your parents are having a barbecue this weekend," Quinn stated as soon as she stepped into his study.

Milo turned in his chair, and Quinn looked at the wall behind him. The plans hadn't changed.

There was still nothing to indicate he saw her as part of his five- or ten-year plan.

Stop it!

Her heart pounded at her brain's warning. She was not going to fall into the trap she'd fallen into so many times. She wasn't going to look for things that might mean she'd get hurt.

She wasn't.

"And I'll bet Gina's bringing that dip I hate. Well, this time, we'll bring our own," Milo said with a rueful shake of his head.

"I already promised we'd bring dessert." She giggled as he threw his hands in the air. Quinn had heard his dip rant several times over the years. She wasn't even sure Gina liked the dip she brought, but she loved seeing Milo act overly put off by it. And Milo enjoyed the show as much as his sister.

What would life have been like if Quinn and Asher had had inside jokes like that? Had made silly games that annoyed their parents but made each other laugh? Had been partners *and* siblings? It would have been a whole different world. A fun world.

If Milo and Quinn had kids, she hoped they'd be friends, too.

The air rushed from Quinn's lungs as she stared at Milo. Children were a topic Quinn had always tried to push to the back of her mind, but whenever she held a newborn, part of her briefly wondered what it would feel like to cuddle her own.

And now, even though she and Milo had only been dating a few weeks, she could already imagine him snuggling with a little one that had her dark hair and his nose. Could imagine him playing games and encouraging their kids to get along and be friends.

"You okay?"

Milo pulled her close and she sank into his heat. Her heart pounded as the desire for a family—her family—nearly overwhelmed her. "I feel like I should be asking you that."

Milo kissed her cheek, but didn't comment.

"Maybe one day I'll have an inside joke with the Russell family, too."

Milo chuckled and dropped a kiss across her temple. "Challenge accepted."

She laughed as she laid her head against his shoulder. It was a simple statement, but she heard her future in it. Her name might not be on any of those boards—yet—but one way or another, she was going to add a few items to those boards. Items that would fulfill both their dreams.

"You look so happy." Milo's mother squeezed his hand as she looked at Quinn.

Quinn was rocking a friend's baby on the porch. He felt his mind start calculating. If he told her he loved her in three weeks, proposed in six months, then they married six months from that, they could be parents in the next three or four years.

He'd almost adjusted his list a few times over the past week. But each time he'd raised his eraser, his hand had refused to move. Quinn had a list of places she wanted to work. Milo had *a* place he needed to work. There had to be a way to reconcile the two, but he hadn't found it yet.

His mother started pulling fruit trays from the refrigerator. She looked out the window over the sink and smiled. A faraway look came over her features as she stared at the gathered mass outside. "I love having everyone here. Love having the entire weekend off."

"It's nice," Milo agreed as he took a sip of his water. Her distant tone sent shivers along his arms, but he didn't know why.

"I want to do it more often." His mother crossed her arms and looked at him.

He looked out the window and grinned. Today had been close to perfect. The weather had been fine, the food delicious. He wasn't sure he could have planned a finer day if he'd had weeks to do it.

Milo shrugged. "Sure. A little more planning might be a good idea. We got lucky this time, but there is no telling when we might all have the day off again. Babies don't generally hold their deliveries for barbecues."

"Sometimes it's nice not to plan." She looked at him and leaned close. "I want to clear my schedule a bit."

Milo looked at his mother. Her smile was bright, but she was bouncing on her heels.

What was going on?

"Meaning?"

"Felix and I are planning to retire."

"Really?" Milo was stunned. His brain clicked through a multitude of responses as it reeled at the news. This couldn't be—his mother and Felix loved their clinic. They'd just started the birthing center. "I'm…" His mouth seemed stuck. "Stunned," he finally managed.

"I know. But we don't want to work for the rest of our lives. And it seems like the right time to start dialing back."

"Wow," Milo breathed out. He'd always seen his mom at the clinic, had always thought of it as hers. He'd never considered that she and Felix would want to move on. In his mind, that was where they belonged. *Always.*

"So, what are you doing about the clinic, the birthing center?" His throat burned, and Milo took a sip of water to force the uncomfortable sensation away. His mother had taken the job at Oceanside Clinic just after his father died. Her professional relationship with Felix had bloomed into friendship that had eventually turned to love. Milo couldn't imagine Oceanside without them. Didn't want to imagine a stranger running such a special place.

"We were hoping you might want to take it over." His mother's eyes shimmered as they looked at him.

He could see the hope in her gaze. The need. She expected him to take it. To want it. And part of him did.

"I know your father would like the idea, too."

The words set his heart racing. He tried to pull on that thread. Tried to imagine what his father might say, but all he could pull up was the trip to Valley General. His dad bending close to him, saying something about running the unit. Even now, with everything his mother had said, the shadowy image sent chills down his back.

"Milo, you are the best person I can think of to run Oceanside Clinic." His mother smiled. "You helped design the birthing center. It should be you."

Why was she making this so difficult?

She rubbed his hand, and hundreds of memories of them working together at Oceanside jumped into his mind. His first and last day, the babies they'd cooed over, the difficult days when everything had gone wrong. He had a lifetime of memories there.

And only one solid one of his dad.

His mother nodded toward the window. "The birthing center needs a head midwife, too." Her eyes were bright. Maybe she'd expected him to scream no immediately. He should put her hope aside and explain his decision, but the words were caught in his throat.

"Nancy only planned to get it off the ground. She's been talking about retirement for the last three years. I'd planned to talk to Quinn about the position—even before I knew you were together. She's perfect for it."

"She is," Milo agreed. His tongue felt tied. He knew Quinn would love being the head midwife at the birthing center, and that she'd excel at it.

"I know you've dreamed of running a big hospital unit—"

"I haven't *just* dreamed of it," Milo interrupted, and immediately felt heat travel up his neck, but he continued. He had to make his mother understand why his answer had to be no. "I feel called to it. Led to it…by dad."

His mother sighed, but she didn't look away. "Are you prepared for everything you will have to sacrifice?" His mother's eyes darted to the back patio.

Turning his head, Milo couldn't stop the smile spreading across his face. Quinn was dancing barefoot in the grass with the neighbor's granddaughter. She was laughing as they spun around, and his heart expanded as she collapsed on the grass with the young girl.

"I'm not going to have to sacrifice anything." Quinn knew about his plans. She'd seen his boards. She knew what a life with him looked like.

Didn't she?

"With the right plan, you can avoid—"

"Life doesn't always care about your plans," his mother snapped. "As you are so fond of saying, babies don't care about schedules, or birthdays or anniversaries. Children don't care that you're on call. They have dance recitals, baseball games, all sorts of activities. As a physician, you are already going to miss some, but if you run a large unit…" She shook her head. "At Oceanside, you and Quinn could control more of your schedule, your life."

Why was she pushing this? How could his mother not understand? "If you could have seen him that day at Valley General, felt what I felt— what I still feel—you'd understand."

"Milo, you are allowed your own dreams." She smiled. It was the look she'd used when he was a kid and she was trying to coax him into finding the right answer on his own.

"This is my dream." Milo shook his head. How could she not understand? Part of him needed this. And it was larger than the unruly piece of his heart that screamed he belonged at Oceanside Clinic.

"Is it?" She stepped closer. "Or are you trying to make up for something that was never your fault?" Her hands trembled, and she wrapped her arms around her waist. "Listen to me. Your father died in a car accident. That was *not* your fault."

"If I hadn't put off my science fair project..." He hated how small his voice sounded. How it made him face the feeling of failure that had never fully left him.

His mother's warmth seeped into his chest. He wasn't sure when she'd reached out to hug him. Still, he let her hold him as the energy and anger drained from him.

Milo blew out a breath. He loved his mother. But the hole his father's death had left could never be filled. That was the way it was with his grief—it never fully went away. He just learned to move around it, to walk with it.

After several minutes, she raised her head and stroked his cheek. "Milo, for the hundredth time, it wasn't about a poster board. And it wasn't about the flowers he went to get because of our fight, either. It was bad timing, and another person's poor decision-making." She held him tightly.

"Your father loved every minute of his life. He loved you and me and Gina. And he understood that you don't get guarantees." She smiled as she looked at Milo. "The last thing he would have wanted was for you to be unhappy."

Milo shook his head. "I'm not unhappy." It was true. He enjoyed his work at St. Brigit's, was looking forward to competing for the Valley General position when it opened. Just because he loved Oceanside didn't mean he had to give up the dream he'd had for so long.

She kissed his cheek. "Your father would have loved Oceanside, too. He sometimes talked about owning his own practice."

"He did?" That revelation stunned him. He racked his brain, but he couldn't think of a single time he'd heard that before.

His mother sighed, and her eyes drifted to the side. "Parents are always more than their children see, at least when they are young." Her hand wrapped around his. "On rough days, your dad even talked about becoming a full-time writer. I always thought he was joking, but there were three unfinished fantasy manuscripts at the bottom of his filing cabinet that I found…" She bit her lip and waved a hand. "The point is, he had many dreams. And he would want you to live yours."

Running the Valley General unit was his

dream…wasn't it? The thing that promised him comfort? The thing he wanted terribly? It was. "My career is in LA."

Her fingers patted his cheek before she turned to grab the fruit platter. "I know that's what your plans say, sweetheart. Just make sure it's what *you* really want." Then she headed back out onto the patio, leaving him alone with his thoughts and memories.

CHAPTER NINE

MILO HAD KISSED her and then disappeared into his study as soon as they got home. Did he know that his mother had talked to her about running the birthing center at the Oceanside Clinic? Surely, she'd discussed it with him. But each time Quinn had tried to broach the topic on the ride home, Milo had changed the subject.

He hadn't even attempted to be subtle about it. She knew he liked working together at St. Brigit's. But he wasn't going to stay there forever. He'd brought up St. Brigit's new hire and the empty spot left at Valley General only once, but she knew how much he wanted that position.

If she accepted Diana's offer, they could live halfway. But that meant at least an hour and a half commute with traffic for each. And if they were on call, it would be easier to stay at the hospital than to come home.

How long could they last living that way?

She preferred the hominess of birthing centers. The personal care she got to give with only having a few women giving birth on any one day. She'd been at hospitals where she'd helped deliver a dozen babies during her shift. There wasn't time to enjoy the newborn's snuggles, to help a new mom acclimate to breastfeeding, or to answer the dozens of questions that arose in the first hours of new life.

None of those needs had gone unseen. But *she* hadn't been able to take her moms from prenatal to postpartum care. And Quinn loved that aspect of the job. It was what put the bounce in her step when she went in for each shift.

Milo loved it, too. Loved watching the joy that came with new life. And he was going to miss it terribly if he ran the ob-gyn unit at Valley General and had to focus much of his time on the minutia of making a unit run well.

Resolved, she started for the study. If they were to have a future together, they needed to get on the same page. And Quinn was done letting him change the topic…and done avoiding it herself.

He didn't turn around as she entered the study. He'd been in here for almost an hour, but none of the tension she'd seen in the car had leaked from him. Whatever was going on, she could help him—talk him through it, like he'd talked her through so many things in the last few weeks alone.

"So, I take it my mother told you that she and my stepfather are planning to retire?"

His voice was distant as she stepped up beside him. Quinn knocked his hip with hers, trying to push a bit of the rigidity from him. "She did. I expect that we shall be getting a lot more barbecue invitations in the future."

He nodded, but his eyes never wavered from the wall before them. "They want me to run Oceanside Clinic when they retire."

The words stunned Quinn. Diana hadn't mentioned that when she'd discussed the midwife job with her. Her heart pounded in her chest. That would solve all the problems she'd been worrying about for the past ten minutes. "Really! That would be perfect. You would be so good—"

"I told her no." Milo's words were flat as they fell between them.

Quinn was shocked. "No? Just no? Without even telling her you'd think about it?" She knew he had his plans. But this was the chance to run his own clinic. A place he loved.

"I don't need to think about it." A nerve twitched in Milo's jaw as he stared at the wall of goals in front of him. "I've already made the necessary decisions about my future," Milo said, gesturing to the words scrawled in front of him.

"Your future?" The words slipped through Quinn's numb lips.

Not *our* future…

Stepping between him and the boards, Quinn waited for Milo to look at her. Her chest was knotted, but her voice was steady. "These are whiteboards. Do you know what is wonderful about them?" She ran her hand across one and held up her finger stained with red ink. "You can figure out what you want and alter the plan."

She trembled as she stared at him. She'd never touched his boards. They were sacred to him. A physical homage to his father. She'd crossed a line, but she couldn't go back now.

Her heart stung as she looked at him. Her parents had been rigid. Milo wasn't a rigid person— he planned, liked to know what he was doing, but he could adjust.

Couldn't he?

"Why can't you even consider changing them for this opportunity?"

"Because I'm not impulsive! Not..." Milo pulled his hand across his face.

"Not flighty. Is that what you mean? Never flying off to parts unknown for a position, right?" Her lips trembled as she wrapped her arms around her waist.

"That wasn't what I was going to say." Milo's voice was firm, but he still wouldn't look at her.

She wanted to challenge him, and her heart ached as he stared at the erased marks on his board. They were just notes, writings that could be replaced.

She waited a moment longer, wishing he'd look at her. Just her. Then she turned. If she spoke, Quinn worried it was going to be something hurtful.

Bottling up the pain pushing through her, she headed for the door. She knew he wouldn't follow her, and that crushed her spirit a bit further. They each needed some time to blow off steam, but she still wished that he would run after her.

Her cell phone rang as she grabbed her keys. She hit Ignore as she walked out. She didn't have a goal in mind—she just needed to be somewhere else.

Anywhere else.

She'd walked through the small park by the apartment three times before her phone rang again. It wasn't Milo's ring, and her heart seized when she saw her old traveling nurse agency's number. Swallowing, Quinn answered. It never hurt to listen, to think about possibilities, to have a backup plan.

A backup plan…

The simple thought crushed her soul. But she pressed Answer on her phone.

"Quinn! I have the perfect position for you!" Isla didn't wait for Quinn to say hello. The staffing adviser was one of the bubbliest individuals Quinn had ever met. "It's in Maine, and you don't have to be there for three months. It's a six-month rotation as the lead of a midwifery unit, while the head midwife is out on maternity leave."

Quinn puffed out a breath. It was as far from Milo as she could get and still remain in the continental US. She looked up at the high-rise complex and rubbed a tear away. "I'm not sure. Can you give me a few days?"

"Of course. But there is actually another position I need to fill, too. Do you know a Sherrie Foster? She works at St. Brigit and applied a few months ago. She's very qualified for the other midwife position at this unit. The traveling nurse there now plans to rotate out in a few months, too."

"She's wonderful." Quinn wrapped an arm around her waist. Sherrie had mentioned applying. Quinn had told her that she'd be a reference, but Sherrie hadn't mentioned it again. "She'd be a good fit for the head position, too, if I decide to turn it down."

Quinn kicked a rock. Could she take the position at Oceanside if she and Milo weren't destined for forever?

No.

The word resounded in her head. Her phone beeped, and she quickly told Isla that she'd let her know in a few days.

Come home...please. Milo's text sent chills racing across her heart. Was it her home? All of this had happened so quickly. And she'd erased part of one of his boards.

What had come over her? Fear.

She wanted Milo to choose her. To rewrite his plans or to at least include her in discussions about the future. She needed to know that he saw her dreams as part of his future, too.

Milo paced back and forth, trying to calm himself. His brain had panicked when Quinn had held up her ink-stained finger. No one erased his boards. They were his connection to his father—erasing them felt almost like betrayal.

But in his frustration, he'd lashed out. Impulsive might not sound like a horrid thing to fling into a conversation, but he'd known how she might take it. And then he hadn't been able to do anything but stare at the blank spaces she'd left. She'd wiped it all away so easily.

How different would his life be if he could do that? And why hadn't he chased after her already?

Milo wanted her home. And with each passing minute, his stomach sank further. He'd gone to the door three times, thinking he'd heard her, only to be met with the curious stare of his neighbor.

He'd called, and she hadn't answered. Then he'd sent the text. He looked at his phone. Quinn had read it twenty minutes ago and hadn't responded. What if he'd driven her away for good? He didn't want to lose Quinn.

Pressing his hand to his forehead, Milo hit Call on his phone again. He heard Quinn's phone ring in the hallway outside and tripped over a shoe in his rush to get to the door. His knees collided with the tiled floor, but Milo didn't care. Quinn was here.

"I am so sorry."

"I'm sorry."

They each said the words at the same time as Quinn rushed to his side. Milo stood, ignoring the pain in his knees as he held her. "I should not have let you think that I thought you impulsive or flighty, and I should have immediately come after you. I am so sorry."

"I shouldn't have wiped away part of your board." Quinn rested her head against his shoulder. "I know how much those mean. I just…" Her words were firm. "I just wanted you to think about it."

Milo stiffened. He had thought about it. Maybe not today, or at least not as much today, but years ago. Even if he wasn't trying to honor his father. Oceanside wasn't what he wanted.

At least, it wasn't the only thing he wanted— was it?

Why did his brain keep coming back to that thought? Milo had charged down this path for years. With the potential opening at Valley General, it was finally within his grasp—finally, he could be close to his dad again.

So why did it feel like his heart was leaning away from it now that the opportunity was here?

"What if I consider it for a few days?" He hadn't meant for the question to exit his mind.

Quinn's eyes met his. An emotion he feared was doubt hovered in them. "I promise to think about it, Quinn. It's just… I've had my career path laid out for years. I swore I'd do this for my dad."

"What about what you want?" Quinn's voice was quiet, but he felt her stiffen in his arms.

Leaning back, he looked at her. Why did his heart have to want so many conflicting things? "Give me a couple of days to think about it."

She smiled, but it wasn't quite full. "That's all I'm asking."

She kissed his cheek, but the fear coating his heart didn't disappear.

Was that really all she was asking? And what if he didn't change his mind?

Milo kept those questions buried inside. She was back—in his arms. That was what mattered tonight.

Milo nodded as he handed Quinn a tablet chart. Dark circles underlined his beautiful eyes, and the strum of tension that had connected them over the last week hummed as her fingers touched his. He grinned, but it was taut. When was the last time she'd seen him smile? Really smile?

They'd always remained professional during work, but the little touches and stolen conversations were gone. There was an uncharted space between them now.

And neither wanted to address it.

Quinn wished there was a way to go back to the early days of their relationship. Then she scoffed. They'd been together less than three months. These *were* the early days.

And if they were already at an impasse?

Since they were teenagers, Quinn had talked to Milo about almost everything. During the first weeks of their relationship, she'd relished how easy it was to talk to him as a partner. To already know his tells.

Now it was a curse. Quinn knew he was stressed. But when she asked about it, he just said it was nothing. And she was hiding things, too. She hadn't taken the job in Maine, hadn't turned it down, either. And she hadn't told Milo—yet. Her heart ached at all the unsaid words between them.

She bit her lip. She and Milo had managed to get through the last few days by ignoring the giant boulder between them. She wanted to run the midwifery unit at Oceanside, and he wanted to be the head of Valley General's obstetrics program.

Were those two things really so at odds?

Quinn tapped a pencil on the nurse's station and tried to catch her breath. Were relationships supposed to be this hard to navigate?

"You okay?" Sherrie asked as she leaned over the nurses' station and placed her tablet on the charging pad.

"Yes." The lie weighed on her heart, but if she opened up about it, Quinn worried that she would burst into tears. Or maybe rage at what she feared were Milo's unyielding dreams.

Sherrie raised an eyebrow, but she didn't press her. "If you decide you want to talk about it, I'm available."

She was pleased by the kind offer. "Thank you."

Her friend nodded. "I suspect Keena will be delivering by the weekend, but Hanna is at least another week away. We might need to start talking about what happens if we need to do an induction."

Quinn smiled as the conversation turned to work. This was an area where she was comfortable. She didn't doubt herself inside these walls. Didn't doubt that she had a place. In the midwifery unit, she knew what to expect and trusted herself.

Babies might keep to their own schedules,

but Quinn knew there were patterns you could recognize, once you'd been a midwife for long enough. "Hanna will not be thrilled with an induction. She's already overdue, and she had to be induced with her first. I remember when she was here for her twelve-week appointment. She wanted to know what she could do to avoid it happening again."

"I know," Sherrie said. "I mentioned it to her today, and her reaction was what you'd expect. After a few sniffles, she squared her shoulders. Pitocin is no one's first choice, but she said whatever is best for the baby."

Quinn smiled. "Right answer. She still has at least another week before we need to start worrying, though. Maybe the little one will grant his mother some grace."

"Maybe." Sherrie turned off her tablet, but she didn't look very confident. "I'm off for the night. And Quinn—" Sherrie crossed her arms "—if you need anything, let me know. I owe you. Particularly if you turn down that head nurse position in Maine."

"They told you they'd offered it to me, huh?" Quinn rolled her eyes. "Isla is bubbly and happy, but she is not known for her discretion. One day it's going to get her in trouble. What if you'd wanted to battle it out with me?" Quinn laughed.

"If you want it, the job's yours. I know that." Sherrie said it with such confidence that Quinn's head popped back. "You've worked all over the place and literally fled a wildfire while successfully delivering a patient. Of course, you're their first choice."

Quinn let out a breath. "My résumé is certainly unique."

"I've never left California. I'm excited about the opportunity." Sherrie swallowed before continuing. "Though it would be nice to know someone in Maine." She waved as she headed toward the employee lounge. "Oh, I didn't see you there, Dr. Russell," Sherrie said as she stepped around Milo—who had appeared at an exam room doorway—and disappeared down the hall.

Milo's face didn't give anything away, but Quinn wrapped her arms around herself as she stared at him.

Had he heard?

Quinn had meant to discuss the Maine offer with him several times, but the tension between them was already high. The time was never right, and the last thing she wanted to do was to make him think she was fleeing. It was just a backup plan—one she wasn't going to use.

She wasn't.

She'd checked his study each day, hoping to see some sort of change on his board, some indication that he saw her as permanent. But nothing had changed. What if she told him about the job offer and he told her to take it? That would make his choice about the Oceanside Clinic and Valley General so much easier.

Before she could gauge his reaction, Tara Siemens walked into St. Brigit's and immediately doubled over, clenching her belly. Quinn and Milo reached her at nearly the same time.

"How far apart are the contractions?" Milo's voice was light, but she could see the small tremor in his jaw. He'd heard Sherrie. Worry cascaded through her, but there wasn't time to deal with it now.

"Five… minutes…" Tara panted. "I tried to get Brandon to come. But he wouldn't answer my calls."

Fury floated across Quinn's skin. It didn't matter what the differences were between Tara and her ex-fiancé—to not answer the call of your pregnant ex when you knew she was close to delivery was horrible. Sucking in a quick breath, Quinn squeezed Tara's hand as Milo led her back to a delivery room.

"My parents are gone, and my sister lives on the other side of the country. She's going to come out for a few weeks next month, but she has two under two so…" Tara looked out the window and wiped away a tear as she rubbed her belly. "Brandon was all I had."

"Well, soon you're going to have a new little

member of the family. And Quinn and I will make sure you are never alone." Milo's voice was soft as he started hooking up the monitor to measure Tara's contractions.

Never alone...

Milo had made the promise so easily. At St. Brigit's or at Oceanside, it could be effortlessly accomplished, but such a promise would be a stretch at a large facility like Valley General.

The buzzer on Quinn's hip went off. "I need to see another patient, but I'll leave you in the capable hands of Dr. Russell for now, and I'll be back shortly."

As Quinn stepped to the door, she glanced back at Milo. He was talking with Tara about movies while watching the monitors, fully focused on his patient, on making sure she'd be okay delivering without a loved one. In a larger facility, he wouldn't have the luxury to take his time like this.

He laughed at something Quinn couldn't hear, and she watched his shoulders relax. A facility like St. Brigit's or Oceanside would make him happiest. It was where he belonged. How could he not see that?

Quinn had been offered a position across the country.

And she hadn't told him.

The thought ricocheted around his mind as he stepped out of Tara's birthing room. He'd managed to trade off care with Quinn during Tara's labor as he wasn't sure how long he could be around her without begging for answers.

Tara smiled as she walked past him. Her contractions had remained five minutes apart for the last two hours, so one of the nursing aids was walking the halls with her now, trying to move labor along.

"I talked to Tara's ex." Quinn's voice was low as she motioned for Milo to follow her into the employee lounge.

His heart leaped as they stepped into the room together. They were at work, but his palms ached to touch her. His arms wanted to pull her close. To kiss away the worry lines marring her forehead. To plead for answers about the Maine job. But none of those things was possible right now.

"You called him?" Milo was stunned. He'd thought Brandon was acting immaturely. Hopefully, he'd change his actions after his child was born. If not before. But there were rules and procedures that had to be followed.

Quinn's eyes widened. "Of course not."

He saw the hurt flash across her features. The words he'd said to her these past few days always seemed to be off. The easiness that had flowed between them had evaporated once the offer to run the Oceanside Clinic had been thrown into the mix. If only she could understand that his plans didn't include a return to Oceanside.

He needed to focus. "Sorry, Quinn." She was an excellent midwife and nurse. She knew the rules regarding patient information.

Her face relaxed a bit, but she didn't touch him. All the little touches, the small smiles, that he'd taken for granted had disappeared. He craved them.

She sighed as she leaned against the bay of lockers. "He's called the admitting desk every thirty minutes since she arrived." Quinn shook her head. "If he's so concerned with her condition, then he should be here...which is what I told him."

Milo let out a soft chuckle. "And how did he take that?"

"Told me they were too different and hung up the phone." Quinn sighed. "Differences may keep them apart, but they are bound by a child forever. Shame he can't see that right now."

"Differences have a way of piling up." Milo's voice was tight. For a moment, he wasn't sure if he was talking about Tara and Brandon or him and Quinn.

Partners didn't have to be exactly the same. But they did need to want the same things. And if she could still consider taking a job with her traveling nursing agency... The thought tore through his soul.

Why hadn't she immediately told her old agency she wasn't interested in the new job?

Quinn's eyes held his, and he could see the questions hovering there. But now wasn't the time to discuss them. Besides, he was terrified of the answers. Terrified that she wouldn't choose his plan.

Wouldn't choose *him.*

"Tara's contractions are picking up." The aid slipped back from the employee lounge door before either Quinn or Milo could respond.

He watched Quinn swallow before he nodded at the door.

"Shall we go see about a baby, Dr. Russell?"

Dr. Russell? He would focus on what that meant later.

"Are you coming to bed?" Quinn rubbed her arms as she stood in the doorway of Milo's study. Tara's labor had finally proceeded, and she'd delivered a healthy baby boy. But she'd been alone. Her ex had answered when she'd asked Milo to call and tell him he had a son, but Quinn didn't know if he would come visit the baby. She hoped he would.

There was so much for Quinn and Milo to talk about, but he'd grabbed a quick snack and retreated almost as soon as they'd arrived home. It stung. He was pulling away from her. And Quinn had no idea how to draw him back.

How did she compete with plans he felt he owed his father?

Should she?

That was the question that tore through her the most.

Life without Milo had never seemed like an option before. They'd sworn when this started to remain friends. Quinn now saw how laughable that was. As if there was a way she could act as though her heart wouldn't always cry out for him.

She loved him. Always would. But if this ended, their friendship would be a casualty. Her heart tore as she stared at his back. "Milo?"

"When were you going to tell me that you were considering moving to Maine?" His voice was rough as he looked over his shoulder.

Quinn went cold as she tried to find the right words. They needed to talk. Needed to figure out what was next.

If anything…

"I should have told you. But they called after our—" her voice caught "—disagreement the other night, and the timing wasn't right." She felt her throat closing, but she pushed through. "I haven't accepted the position."

"Have you turned it down?" His voice was rough—*hurt*.

"No." Quinn bit her lip, wishing there was a different answer, but it was the truth. "I always think about job offers for a few days." That was her routine. He knew that. She'd always talked to him about where the agency had open positions and gotten his thoughts, though he'd commented more than once that she always went with her gut, so why ask him?

"So what does your gut say you should do? Is the job calling to you more than LA?" The lines around Milo's eyes were deep as he dug his fingers into his folded arms.

"That is *not* fair," Quinn shot back. They were exhausted, too exhausted to have this argument now. "We should get some rest, then we can discuss the Oceanside Clinic, Maine, and everything else."

"I'm not going to take my mom's offer. It's not what I want."

What about what she wanted? What about their future—together?

She had wanted to put off for a few more hours what now felt inevitable. It would be his plan that mattered. His choice that reigned.

"We need to figure out our plan."

"Now, it's *our* plan?" Quinn wanted to shake him. She'd wanted him to start including her in his plan weeks ago. For a man who plotted everything out, she should have seen some sort of change on his whiteboards. Or some mention of their future. So where was she? Where was her place amid his dreams of running Valley General's OB unit?

And if she stayed, would he keep looking at her like she was a flight risk? "Are you expecting me to leave? Ever since Terri offered me the position in Orlando, I feel like you've been waiting for me to say I'm packing my bags."

Milo shrugged, and Quinn felt her heart crack.

"I've been looking for the signs that you're about to leave ever since you moved back. That's what you do, Quinn. You leave. But me? I can't go anywhere. The job for senior OB at Valley General opened yesterday."

So, she hadn't been the only one keeping career opportunities secret.

"And if you don't get it?"

"I will," Milo stated.

To be so confident…

"But if you don't, will you consider your mother's opportunity then?" Pain dug into her palms and she forced her fingers to relax.

"If I don't get it, then I'll look at Mercy General. Valley hires out of there regularly."

Pain ripped through her as she looked at his infernal boards. He'd never thought she was staying—no wonder Milo hadn't adjusted his plans to include her.

Instead, he'd painstakingly rewritten the words her hand had erased two days ago. Though the ink looked different. Her heart sank as she stared at it.

Why didn't it have the silky look of Dry Erase markers?

Stepping up to the board, she ran her finger along it. It came away clean.

She held it up for his inspection. "I was a traveling nurse for more than a decade. It was a job I loved, but I never considered leaving St. Brigit's until you refused to even consider Oceanside Clinic. To consider something different, some other way to honor your father, your dreams, and mine. It doesn't just have to be Valley General, Milo."

"If you had seen his face, Quinn. Felt what I felt—what I still feel. I know objectively that my actions weren't the reason he passed. But I need this, and it is within my reach. If not now, then in a few years."

How did one compete with a ghost?

"I need this."

More than he needed her?

Quinn couldn't ask that question. Couldn't bear the answer.

Her hand shook as she pointed at the boards.

"I understand, but these aren't *our* plans, Milo. They're yours. And in the last forty-eight hours, the only change you've made to them is to write the notes in permanent marker."

Quinn closed her eyes and rocked back on her heels. "If this isn't what I want, then I don't fit in to these plans, do I? My desire to run a unit, Oceanside..." Her lip trembled, but she refused to break. Not yet. There would be plenty of time for that later. *Forever.*

"Of course you fit in. You love being at St. Brigit's. And you'd love Mercy General or Valley General." Milo's nose scrunched as he looked at her.

"So, if I make all the adjustments. Change all my plans..." Quinn shuddered.

How come her dreams were so easy to dismiss?

And why was this happening with Milo? The one person who knew her better than anyone.

"You go from position to position, trusting your gut." Milo stared at her. "That isn't a plan."

She'd had a lot of positions over the last decade, but each one had added a valuable piece to her résumé. And each had taught her what she really wanted, and it wasn't to be another face in a large hospital.

"Trusting my intuition on job choices doesn't mean that I don't think things through. Just because I don't need to list out every move for the next five or fifty years doesn't make my choices less valid. It doesn't mean I don't know what I want." Quinn brushed away the lone tear that refused to listen to her mandate.

"I want to belong, to be chosen. For who *I* am. I don't want someone who has to fit me in. I want a man who stands beside me and sees me and my dreams in his future. Who is willing to change his plans if it's what's best for us." Quinn stared at him, willing him to change his mind. To say he wanted her. No matter what.

"Your dreams matter to me. But I need this. I need Valley General," Milo countered, and the final piece of hope died inside her.

"Why? It's just a place. Why does it have to be the only place?" Pain tumbled through her, but she needed an answer.

"I've thought about it for years. I've researched everything." He pushed a hand through his hair.

It wasn't an answer, not really. But she'd heard similar words before, so many times.

Our plan is best, Quinn. We've done all the research and work, so you don't have to. Why can't you just get in line?

"Where do I fit on that list, Milo? Or your family? Or children? What if we don't fall in line with the plan?" Quinn gestured to the boards.

Love, real love, didn't ask you to adjust for it. It accepted you.

"Life can't be outlined like a book. Chaos and change are inevitable." Her heart wept as she stared at him. It had to be this way, but she hated it.

She wished she'd paid more attention to the last time they'd kissed. Wished she could remember the last time he'd held her more clearly. If she'd known it had been the last time, she'd have made sure to let it seep into every edge of her soul.

Pushing the pain away for a moment longer, she met his gaze. "I want you to get everything on your list, Milo. I really do." She tried to force out a goodbye, but her heart refused to provide any words as it broke.

She turned without looking back. If she looked at him, she'd break.

If he had chased after her, she'd have pledged whatever he'd wanted. But he hadn't. He'd stayed in the study while she'd packed the small number of belongings she'd accumulated during their relationship, the door firmly closed to her dreams and wishes.

She hung her key on the ring by the kitchen and forced her eyes to stare ahead as she closed the front door behind her. It was time to move on. To find the next adventure, even if it never excited her as much as these last few months with Milo had.

CHAPTER TEN

MILO SAT ON the floor of his living room and stared at the bright yellow kitchen as the sun rose. He'd spent the entire night trying to figure out how everything had gone so wrong. How his deepest dream had evaporated in a matter of minutes.

He looked at the small box on the coffee table. After Quinn had left the study, he'd stared at the window, trying to find the right words to explain why he'd rewritten everything in permanent marker. To explain that after his mother had offered him the chance to run Oceanside, he'd rewritten it so he couldn't change his mind. So, it wouldn't seem like an option to derail him from his father's memory. It was ridiculous and childish. But Milo had felt better after the small gesture.

Then he'd stared at the boards rather than run after her. Trying to find an adjustment, so they both got what they needed. A way that didn't feel like he was letting down his father or Quinn. But nothing had come to him.

Finally, he'd grabbed the box from the drawer where he'd hidden it weeks ago. He hadn't planned to buy it. It had happened by accident. *By impulse.* He'd walked past the jewelry store and had just been pulled in.

But after the purchase, he'd started second-guessing himself. Wondering if it had been too soon. If he should have spent more time research-ing to find the perfect symbol of his devotion. He'd spent so much time worrying over it that he hadn't even managed to figure out the best plan for asking the woman he loved to be his wife.

And then he'd been unable to give her what she'd really wanted—needed—when she'd asked. A chance to be included in his future—fully. Her dreams and his, blended in harmony.

He'd wanted her, but on his terms. By the time he'd grabbed the ring—the symbol that he wanted her forever—Quinn was already gone. And she hadn't answered any of his calls or texts since.

He didn't blame her. Quinn had only wanted to know that she was part of his life. That she'd have a say on their future. And he'd dismissed her dreams. Dismissed her gut feelings.

Dismissed the woman he loved.

He'd clung to an idealized version of a memory and lost the person that made him happiest as a result. And now he had no idea where she was.

Milo laid his head back against the couch and tried to force air through his lungs. She was gone, and he was alone. Everything hurt.

How was he supposed to get through the rest of his life without Quinn? From the moment they'd met, he'd felt like she was family. She'd been his constant. A place of sanctuary. His person. Why hadn't those words materialized when they'd been arguing?

Fear.

Milo pressed his palms against his closed eyes. As soon as she'd landed in LA, Milo had been afraid that Quinn would leave. Feared that he wouldn't be able to compete with the adventures she'd already had and could have in the future. She wanted to work at Oceanside now, but what if, in a few years, another phone call came, offering something even more exciting?

He pressed his palm to his forehead. He had spent all his time calculating how she might leave…but what if she stayed? Milo had never fully considered that. And he'd never forget the look in her eyes when he'd confessed that he'd been looking for signs that she'd leave for almost a year—or the selfish hope that had wanted her to promise that she wouldn't. Relationships took adjustments, but other than painting his kitchen, what adjustments had he made for her?

None! his brain shouted. He'd held back, hoping she'd make all the changes. That way, he wouldn't have to examine what he really wanted. What he really needed. He could just float by on the path that he thought might bring him some form of closure with his dad.

Even if he wasn't sure it was what he really wanted.

God, Quinn was right to leave.

He dialed her number again and bit his lip as the call immediately went to voice mail. What had he expected? She'd asked to have a say in the dreams they followed, and he'd stayed silent, terrified to embrace a future that might mean letting go of the past.

He called St. Brigit's. He wasn't on shift today, but he needed to take some additional personal time. He couldn't see Quinn. At least not yet.

Not until I have a *plan.* The thought ran through his mind, and Milo wanted to bang the rigidity out of his brain.

He'd lost Quinn because of his incessant need to organize his life, to pretend he had some say in life's chaos. Yet, that was where his brain wanted to go, wanted to leap to: the security of plans.

Except nothing in his plans had prepared him for such heartbreak.

He called HR and asked for two weeks off. He doubted his heart would ever heal, but maybe by then the simple act of forcing oxygen into his lungs wouldn't be so difficult.

Standing, he ignored the pain in his legs. He'd been on the floor for too long, but Milo didn't care. He couldn't stay here, couldn't be where everything reminded him of Quinn. Grabbing his keys, he raced for the door. He didn't have a destination in mind, but anywhere had to be better than the emptiness here.

Quinn stared at the gray walls of her hotel room. When had gray become such a popular color? At least the sad color matched the feel of her soul. The hotel was the first one she'd passed after leaving last night. It wasn't much, but with the rental insurance from the fire and staying with Milo, her nest egg was quite healthy.

Milo…

Her lungs burned, but her eyes were finally dry. No matter what she did, his name kept popping into her mind. Even now, it felt like he was everywhere. Milo had seeped into her soul years ago, and there was no way to remove him. No matter how much it hurt.

Her phone rang, but it wasn't Milo's ringtone. Milo had called repeatedly after she left, but Quinn hadn't trusted herself to answer. As soon as she'd closed the door to the apartment, she'd wanted to turn around. Wanted to say that it didn't matter that his life plan was written in permanent ink—without her—she could accept it.

But she couldn't. She'd lived like that before, and she hadn't been able to bend enough to fit. If Milo ever looked at her like her parents had, like she was intruding...

She wasn't sure she could survive it. It was better to leave before that happened. Quinn tasted blood, and belatedly realized that she was biting the inside of her cheek.

Milo wanted a different dream. It wasn't wrong, and he should have it because he'd worked so hard to make sure it happened. She just hoped it brought him all the peace he sought, and wished she'd realized that he would never walk away from his dream before she'd lost her heart so completely.

Each time she heard his ringtone, she'd burst into tears, wishing he'd leave her be. When the calls had stopped, she'd cried again. Nothing felt right anymore.

The phone rang again, and she flipped it over. Her fingers froze, but she managed to answer just before it shifted to voice mail.

"Asher?" Quinn kept her voice level.

"Quinn." Asher's voice was rigid, and immediately she knew something was wrong.

"What's wrong?"

"Samantha's been hospitalized. They're trying to stop her labor." Asher let out a soft whimper. "She's only twenty-two weeks along. If she delivers…" Asher's voice broke.

"Where are you?" Quinn slid from the hotel bed. They weren't close, but she could hear the pain in his voice. And Samantha would be understandably terrified.

"Valley General," Asher stated. "You don't have to come." But she could hear the plea in his voice.

"I'm on my way."

"I think you probably don't need me anymore." Quinn stood and stretched. The hours had passed in a stream of nurses, monitors and checks. The doctor had decided Samantha would spend at least the next two days being monitored, and then be on strict bed rest for the rest of her pregnancy. But, at last, it seemed like Samantha was out of danger.

"Thank you so much for coming," Samantha said as she held out a hand. "Asher, why don't you see Quinn to her car?"

Quinn started to protest, but she caught a look between the two and held her tongue. She and Milo had been able to do that, too. To communicate so much with just a small look.

Her heart bled as she started for the door. Focusing on Asher and Samantha's issues had allowed her a brief respite from her own brokenness. The idea of heading back to her small hotel room held no appeal, but staying here didn't seem like an option, either. Quinn had hovered long enough.

She let her brother follow her to the waiting room then turned to him. "I know that Samantha wanted you to see me out, but it's really okay, Asher. If you have any questions about bed rest or what to expect, you can call."

"I should have called you back." Asher's voice was low as he stared at her. His lip stuck out, and he sighed. "Should have jumped at the chance to have dinner or coffee."

Quinn's heart twisted as she looked at him. It would be easy to offer a platitude. To tell him that it was fine that he'd left her wondering what she'd done wrong and waiting patiently for a response that never came. But her heart wasn't in it. "So why didn't you?"

Her brother pursed his lips before he stuck his hands into his pockets. "I started to, so many times. But I had no idea how to say all that needed to be said. That should be said." Asher rocked back on his heels. "No matter how Mom and Dad tried to change you, you resisted. They tried to mold you into their image, and you refused." Asher ran a hand through his short hair. "You're my hero."

Quinn felt her mouth fall open. Hero? None of that made any sense. "Asher, I think you're remembering everything a bit wrong."

His cheeks heated as he shook his head, "No, I'm not. I gave in to everything they wanted. It was easier—God knows they rewarded me for it—but even after they passed…" He pushed a hand through his hair again. "I became a lawyer just like they wanted me to. Did so many things because—" his lip trembled as he met his gaze "—I didn't know who I was until a few years ago."

His eyes burned through her, but Quinn had no idea what to say.

"You were yourself. No matter how Mom tried to make you blend in, you stood out. You figured out what you wanted in life and left to get it."

"Sure of myself? I was terrified." Quinn shook her head. She'd never felt like she belonged. "I literally ran away."

"Could have fooled me," Asher lightly scoffed. "You set off on an adventure. And then another. And another… I was always in awe of your ability to escape. You never needed anyone."

Never needed anyone? The words struck her. She'd needed Milo, but had she ever told him that? The world spun around her as she tried to steady herself.

Her brother continued. "You see what you want and you go for it. No matter where it means you have to go."

She'd loved being a travel nurse, loved going new places. But it had been lonely, too. Never staying in one place, keeping people at a distance because you weren't sure you'd ever see them again. That was one of the reasons she'd come back to California.

To Milo.

She'd never said it was permanent, though. Milo had been waiting for her to pack her bags because she'd always packed them before.

Even her furniture had been rented.

But she hadn't wanted to get away from Milo.

Had she ever told him that? Ever told him that he was what grounded her, gave her the roots she desperately needed?

No.

Because she'd wanted him to change first. Wanted him to adjust his plans for her, rather than seeing if there was a way they could join their dreams together. Blood rushed through her ears as she tried to focus on her brother.

Asher's warm hand pressed into hers. "I just didn't know how to say how sorry I was for not standing up to Mom and Dad. For just following the safety of the plans laid out before me."

He huffed out a deep breath. "I was jealous of you."

"Jealous?"

He smiled. "When Mom and Dad said they wouldn't pay for nursing school, you told them that you'd already filled out the paperwork for scholarships and applied for a loan. I was in awe of your courage. You set a goal and didn't let anyone distract you or talk you out of it."

Like wanting to run the birthing center at Oceanside. She'd decided that was her next goal—her next adventure. And yet, when Milo hadn't immediately altered everything, she'd run.

Just like he'd feared she would.

But Milo wasn't her parents. His plans hadn't been designed to trap her. *She'd* set that trap, and stepped into it herself.

She knew how important plans were to him. How safe they made him feel. How they brought him closer to his father's memory. Yet she'd asked him to change everything. And it had cost her the person who made her feel whole.

Quinn's heart melted as she embraced her brother. "None of this is your fault. We each made mistakes, but that's in the past now." She meant the words. They'd been children in a home with impossible rules. And each had adapted in their own way. She was too old to keep running from past pains.

"I know it's selfish," Asher said, "but I kind of hope you're planning to stay in the area. At least for a little while. I'd love for our child to spend as much time as possible with Aunt Quinn."

Her heart pounded as she nodded. "I've actually been thinking of making my California residency permanent." The words felt right. She smiled as her brother beamed.

* * *

The Oceanside Clinic had four cars in the employee parking lot as he pulled in. But none of them belonged to his mother or Felix. At least he wouldn't have to immediately explain why he was there.

He'd driven here without thinking. But when he'd finally arrived in Oceanside, Milo hadn't wanted to go to his town house. The memory of Quinn kissing him there was imprinted on his brain. Instead, he'd sat on the beach, just thinking until the sun had finally started to sink over the ocean.

Kelly, the nurse at the front desk, smiled as he walked through the front door. "Dr. Russell." She started to stand, but he motioned for her to stay where she was. "We don't have any patients in labor, two patients and their little ones are sleeping, and Dr. Acton is on call. It's her last month before she moves." Kelly stopped chatting. "Sorry, slow night shift."

"I understand. The shifts drag when there's no one to help. I…" He looked at the pictures he'd helped his sister pick out. "I just needed to see this place."

The words left his mouth and he felt a weight lift from his chest. He needed to walk through this center he'd helped design, needed a chance to say goodbye.

Kelly gave him a strange look, but she didn't say anything as he started down the hall.

Once his mother and Felix retired, he doubted the new physician would want to keep him on as a very part-time employee. His head hurt as he realized he would no longer have a connection to the place.

The thought that this would be someone else's pride and joy felt like a rock in his stomach. His mother and Felix had supported the idea of the birthing center, but it had been Milo's baby. He'd pored over the architect's plans, spent hours researching and investigating how to let mothers birth in complete comfort.

The door to his mother's office was open, and Milo slipped through it. This could be his. *Should be his.*

The thought held him, and Milo exhaled. Peace settled through him. His father wasn't at Valley General. His dad was with him no matter where he served, because Milo carried him with him always. Memories faded, but love carried through time and space. Why had it taken him so long to see that? To accept it?

His cell buzzed, and he smiled as he answered. "I'm surprised it took Kelly this long to let you know I was here."

"Is everything okay?" His mother's voice was tired, but he knew she'd come to the clinic if he said he needed it.

"No," Milo answered honestly. "But it will be. I'm going to run this clinic, Mom."

"And Quinn?"

Just her name was enough to make the blood rush to his ears as his heart ached. He swallowed as he stared across the hall at the office that should be hers. "If I can convince her, this will be our greatest adventure."

"If anyone can figure out a plan for that, it's you."

Milo smiled. "Maybe. But I need a favor."

"Name it!"

He could see his mother's smile in his mind. He hoped that he hadn't pushed Quinn too far. That she'd want to take this new path with him.

CHAPTER ELEVEN

"Why is Milo not on the schedule for the next two weeks?" Quinn's soul shuddered as she looked at Martina. He wasn't supposed to be on the schedule today, and she'd been grateful for the extra day to figure out how to tell him she was staying. And that she wanted to be with him, no matter what his plans were.

She'd turned down the position in Maine last night. For years, Quinn had picked up and moved on when life got tough. She'd controlled life by running from hurt. When she'd faced setbacks, she'd reached for the comfort of knowing that she could escape. But her heart didn't want an escape. There was nowhere better than wherever Milo was. Quinn Davis was done running. She was putting down roots.

The news that Milo was taking an extended vacation had been the talk of the employee lounge when she'd arrived this morning, everyone wondering what he was doing and commenting on the fact that he never normally took leave. She'd caught more than a few side glances her direction, too—though no one had worked up the courage to ask her directly if she knew where he was.

Thank goodness.

"He called in yesterday and asked for some leave." Martina leaned closer. "I bet he's interviewing for the position over at Valley General. If he gets it, he has a lot of unused leave he's accumulated here that he either uses or loses."

"Valley General." Quinn nodded. "Of course."

Martina held up her hands. "I suspect he'll get it. I still remember him telling me his five-year plan during his interview. That man had it all outlined—even then." She shook her head. "I've already put out a few feelers. But if you know anyone who might be interested—send me their name. Oh, and we need to start thinking about your contract, too. We would love to retain you. Let's set up a meeting next week to go over the details."

"I'll get it on your calendar." Quinn smiled.

Her phone buzzed and she froze as Milo's name jumped across the screen.

You left something at my place. Can you come by after your shift?

Left something? Quinn wasn't sure what he'd found, but it couldn't have been anything major. Was this his way of trying to talk…or of pushing the last remnants of her from his life?

I'll be there as soon as my shift ends.

She hit Send and then forced herself to focus on work. Time would move faster if she stayed as busy as possible.

The knock at the door sent tingles across Milo's skin. Quinn was here. She was finally here.

When he'd sent the text this morning, Milo had been prepared to wait exactly one day for her to respond before he took more drastic measures to seek her out. But she'd answered almost instantly. He'd wrapped his mind around all the potential outcomes this afternoon, but he was not going to focus on those now.

Sliding the door open, he took her in. She wore jeans and a loose T-shirt. Her dark hair was pulled into a low ponytail. His body ached with relief as his eyes drank her in.

Quinn…

"Are you going to invite me in?" Her voice wavered a little as she looked past him.

"Oh my gosh!" Milo jumped to the side. "Yes, of course. It's just so good to see you. My brain stopped working." Her lips tipped up, and Milo released the breath he'd been holding. "I was worried you might change your mind about coming."

Her dark eyes raked across him.

Did she want to touch him as much as he wanted to touch her? He refused to examine that thought. There was too much to say.

"You said I left something." Her head swiveled as she looked around the living room. "Where is it?"

"Here." Milo placed a hand to his chest as he let the words flow. "You left my heart."

Milo stepped toward her, grateful when she didn't move away. "It's yours, Quinn, and it always will be. I should have said so many things the other night. I should have promised you forever. I thought my plans grounded me, but they were just a cover for my fear that everything can be ripped away. My life has revolved around plans and control since Dad died. They were my talisman—my protection against the world of unknowns. And my way to keep him close." Milo swallowed, waiting for the grief he always felt when he thought of his dad, but it didn't overwhelm him this time.

"That's understandable."

"Maybe." Milo reached for her hand, unable to keep from touching her. Her fingers wrapped through his, but there was still so much to say.

"But I can't lose my dad—he's part of me. And I never meant to make you feel like you weren't part of my future. *You* are my plan, Quinn.

"I know you like to travel—" Milo let go of her hand to trace his fingers across her chin "—but I'm hoping that I can convince you to stay local. I love it here. Love being close to Mom and Felix and Gina. Even if she does make the worst vegetable dip in history. But if you need—"

"I owe you an apology, too." Quinn closed the bit of distance between them as she interrupted.

"No."

Her finger landed against his lips. "Let me finish."

Milo nodded as he relished the heat from her other hand slipping into his. His heart steadied as Quinn held him. For the first time in two days, the pressure in his chest finally evaporated.

"You were right." Quinn pressed her lips to his cheek. "Maine was my backup." A tear ran down her cheek. "After I wiped away your plans…" She sucked in a breath. "I worried that maybe I wouldn't fit into your life. Wouldn't have a place. And I panicked. But I'm done running."

He pulled her close and just held her. Pressing light kisses to the top of her head, Milo waited until she looked up at him. Pushing the tears from her cheek, Milo held her gaze. "I will always choose you, Quinn. Always."

Then his lips captured hers, and her arms wrapped around his neck as she deepened the kiss.

"I love you, Quinn Davis."

"I love you, too."

He got down on one knee and smiled as her fingers covered her lips. "I bought this weeks ago. When you asked me to show you that your dreams were part of my future, I should have pulled this from the drawer and gotten down on one knee then. You are my plan, Quinn. From now until forever, please say you'll be my wife."

Lowering herself to her knees, Quinn put her hands on either side of his face as she dropped a kiss against his lips. "Yes. Yes." She giggled as he placed the diamond on her finger. "It's perfect."

"There is one other thing we need to discuss. About St. Brigit's…"

"Martina mentioned my contract today. And that you might be taking a position at Valley General." Quinn squeezed his hand.

"You didn't sign a new contract, did you?" Milo's voice was rushed, and he shook his head. "It's just, I made one plan without talking to you. Well—two, but that's all. I promise."

Quinn raised an eyebrow. "What have you done?"

"After you left, I couldn't stay here. I went to

Oceanside. I meant to say goodbye to the facility, but..." Milo smiled. "It's where I belong. I want to run the clinic and the birthing center. Do you want to run the midwife unit?"

"Yes!" Quinn's scream echoed in the room, and she covered her lips. "That was a little loud!"

"I loved it." Milo kissed her. "But there is still the other plan."

Quinn's brow furrowed, but she didn't interrupt him.

"I got my mother and Felix to agree to put off their retirement for six months." Milo pushed a loose piece of hair behind her ear.

"Why?" Quinn's eyes were wide as she stared at him.

"In case you wanted to go on one more tour with Doctors Without Borders. You mentioned getting away a few weeks ago. Once we take over the clinic, that option will not be something we can do—at least not without a lot of pre-planning. And if we have a family, then it becomes even harder."

"We?" Quinn's voice was low as she ran her hand along his cheek.

"Figure it might be a good time for an adventure."

Milo's heart exploded as she launched into his arms.

"I love you!" She peppered his face with kisses.

EPILOGUE

QUINN BREATHED THROUGH her contractions as she smiled at Robin. She'd been walking with the young woman down Oceanside's hallways for the last hour, hoping it might speed up Robin's contractions. But all it appeared to have done was bring on Quinn's. When she'd said she planned to work up until she delivered, she hadn't meant it so literally.

She looked toward the clock and frowned. The last three had been exactly five and a half minutes apart.

Milo strolled through the front door of the birthing center as she and Robin rounded the nurses' station. He grinned before stepping aside and letting Kelly through, too. Neither of them was supposed to be on rounds today.

"Who told on me?" Quinn squinted as Kelly took Robin's arm.

"So, you are in labor?" Robin grinned.

"I run to the restroom for five minutes…"

Quinn sighed. "I thought I was covering it well, too."

Robin let out a sheepish laugh. "You squeezed my arm almost every seven minutes, then every six. At least our little ones will have the same birthdays." She laughed again before a contraction overtook her.

"I was going to call you as soon as I hit five minutes." Quinn beamed as Milo dropped a kiss on her forehead.

"Right now, all I can think about is that our daughter will be here soon. I brought the birthing bag." Milo's smile spun up her spine as he held up the bag.

They'd packed it weeks ago. Actually, he'd packed it—carefully going over each item on his list. Quinn had laughed and said all they really needed was an outfit for the baby and car seat, but he'd insisted.

"I think this little one is a bit anxious." Quinn gripped Milo's arm as she breathed through another contraction. "Her due date isn't for another three days. She isn't following the plan."

Milo laughed before he kissed her. "Some plans are meant to be broken."

* * * * *